Dear Reader,

I love beginnings! I especially love beginnings that involve cowboys and the women who love them. Welcome to Thunder Mountain Brotherhood! I've been excited about this series from the moment I envisioned a ranch that once housed foster boys. As they learned to ride and rope, they also learned the cowboy code of integrity, courage and loyalty.

Now grown men, they share a love of Thunder Mountain Ranch and a bond stronger than if they'd been born brothers. This summer you'll meet three of them, starting with Cade Gallagher. I can't wait for you to meet Cade, and Lexi, the unforgettable woman he left behind.

I can't wait for you to meet all of them, in fact! None of these guys had an easy start in life, and they have scars both inside and out. That makes them challenging to love, but I have a hunch you'll end up falling for them as quickly as I did.

For those of you who enjoyed my Sons of Chance series, rest assured that you'll see glimpses of those characters, because I couldn't abandon them completely! I predict you'll have fun watching them pop up now and then. In the meantime, come with me to Thunder Mountain Ranch and let me introduce you to some very hot cowboys. We're going to have a great time this summer!

Enthusiastically yours,

Vicki Lewis Thompson

Vicki Lewis Thompson

Midnight Thunder

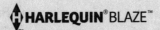
HARLEQUIN® BLAZE™

Recycling programs
for this product may
not exist in your area.

ISBN-13: 978-0-373-79851-3

Midnight Thunder

Copyright © 2015 by Vicki Lewis Thompson

Printed in U.S.A.

www.Harlequin.com

A passion for travel has taken *New York Times* bestselling author **Vicki Lewis Thompson** to Europe, Great Britain, the Greek isles, Australia and New Zealand. She's visited most of North America and has her eye on South America's rainforests. Africa, India and China beckon. But her first love is her home state of Arizona, with its deserts, mountains, sunsets and—last but not least—cowboys! The wide-open spaces and heroes on horseback influence everything she writes. Connect with her at vickilewisthompson.com, facebook.com/vickilewisthompson and twitter.com/vickilthompson.

Books by Vicki Lewis Thompson

HARLEQUIN BLAZE

The Sons of Chance Series

To get the inside scoop on Harlequin Blaze and its talented writers, be sure to check out blazeauthors.com.

All backlist available in ebook format.

Visit the Author Profile page at Harlequin.com for more titles.

To Kathleen Scheibling for believing in me and this series. Let it also be noted that she selflessly braved the rigors of a cover shoot with bare-chested cowboys. What devotion to the cause!

Prologue

CARRYING THEIR BOOTS, Cade Gallagher and Damon Harrison crept out of the ranch house's front door as the grandfather clock in the living room struck twelve. Breaking the house rules was serious, but in this case it was necessary.

After shutting the front door carefully, Cade avoided the porch board that squeaked as he walked over to the steps and sat down to put on his boots.

Damon lowered himself to the top step. "You got your knife?" His voice cracked a little because it was still changing.

"Yep." Cade's voice had changed months ago, and he had to shave every two days now. "You got the matches?"

"Yep."

Cade pulled on his boots and stood. "Ready?"

"Yep."

After taking the steps slow so he wouldn't make too much noise, Cade started toward a grove of trees beyond the main corral. They'd picked out the spot a week ago but had waited for the full moon. It was playing hide-

and-seek with the clouds tonight, but the clouds hadn't dumped any rain, thank God.

After reaching the small clearing, Cade scanned the area. He was the first foster boy taken in by the Padgetts, and he'd used his seniority to claim a leadership position. Damon hadn't bucked him on it. "Looks okay. Nobody's messed with our campfire."

"Nope." Damon produced the matches, lit one and touched it to the small pile of dry leaves and branches they'd heaped in a circle of dirt surrounded by stones. The branches caught instantly.

"We need to make this quick." Cade sat crosslegged on the ground. After opening his pocket knife, he dipped the blade into the flames. "It won't burn for long."

Damon held out his palm. "Do it."

"Maybe you should do your own."

"No, you." He squeezed his eyes shut and shoved his hand toward Cade.

So Damon was scared. Cade thought about asking if he wanted to forget the whole thing, but Damon wouldn't like the suggestion that he was a wimp. Cade had never sliced into someone before, but this had been his idea, so he had to hang tough. Taking a deep breath, he grabbed his friend's hand and made a small cut across the base of his thumb. Blood oozed out.

Damon winced and kept his eyes closed. He looked a little pale, but that might have been because of the moonlight.

Letting go of Damon's hand, Cade held his own palm steady and applied the knife to the same spot. It hurt, but nothing like the beatings he used to get from his old man. "Okay. I'm ready."

Damon opened his eyes. "We're supposed to say something, but I don't think I remember it all."

"That's okay. I've got it." He positioned their hands so the cuts were aligned. "Just hold on." As Damon gripped his hand, Cade said the words they'd written down and he'd memorized.

"On Thunder Mountain Ranch in the state of Wyoming, we swear to be straight with everyone and protect the weak. Bound by blood, we declare ourselves the Thunder Mountain Brotherhood. Loyalty above all."

"What you guys doing out here?"

They both cussed and scrambled to their feet as Finn O'Roarke walked into the clearing. He'd come to the ranch two weeks ago and was still feeling his way. He was only a little younger than Damon and Cade, but he seemed more like a kid.

Cade found his voice first. "Damn it, Finn! Don't ever sneak up on a guy like that. I could've knifed you!"

Finn narrowed his eyes. "You're not supposed to be out here. House rules."

"Hell, we know that," Damon said. "But we had business to attend to."

"And now you're blood brothers." In the flickering light, Finn's expression revealed longing mixed with hesitation.

Cade was a sucker for that look. He remembered all too well how it felt to be an outsider who didn't have the nerve to ask to be included. He glanced at Damon. They'd been talking about this for a long time, before Finn ever showed up. They'd decided being blood brothers would be cool, maybe even cooler than if they'd had the same parents.

But now here was Finn, who would probably be

thrilled to be part of it. Cade couldn't blame him. It
had to be hard to show up at a foster home and the other
guys were already friends. Cade lifted his eyebrows and
hoped Damon would get the silent request.

Damon sighed. "Yeah, fine."

Cade looked over at Finn. "You want to be a blood
brother with us?"

"I wouldn't mind." His attempt to sound casual was
a total failure.

"You have to cut your hand. Or let me do it."

Finn's jaw tightened. "I'll do it."

Cade wanted to laugh but didn't dare. Finn didn't
know that Damon had been too scared to cut his own
hand, but Cade wasn't about to rat on his new blood
brother. He handed the knife, handle first, to Finn.

"Where do I cut?"

"Here." Cade held his palm out.

"Okay." The kid might seem young, but he had balls.
He made the cut. "Now what?"

"Press your hand to mine while I say the words.
Then do it again with Damon. That way you're bonded
with both of us."

Finn was a whiz at following directions. In seconds
the thing was done.

The flames had nearly gone out, but Cade was taking
no chances they'd start a forest fire. He scooped up a
handful of loose dirt. "We need to smother it real good."

Finn and Damon helped him pile more dirt on it.
They made a pretty big mound. Starting a fire in the
woods would get them all sent away, possibly to some
juvenile detention center. Cade couldn't speak for the
other two, but he sure as hell didn't want that. Thunder Mountain Ranch was his best bet, and he knew it.

Finn threw another handful of dirt on the fire. "I heard what you said both times, but what does it actually mean, being in this brotherhood thing?"

Damon groaned. "*Now* you ask."

"That's okay." Cade felt the need to stick up for the kid, who was braver than he looked. "He wasn't in on the planning stages." He turned to Finn. "It means we won't lie or steal, and we won't let anybody get bullied."

"All right. That's cool."

"And we're brothers, so of course we'd give our life for each other."

Finn sucked in a breath. "Really? Like dying?"

"Hey, it probably won't ever be necessary, but that's the bottom line. Mostly it means we'll stick together. Watch out for each other. Be friends forever."

"Oh." Finn smiled. "I'm okay with that."

The moon picked that moment to come out from behind a cloud and shine down on them again. It seemed like a sign to Cade, but he didn't want things to get too mushy. "Yeah. Me, too. And now we'd better get our asses back in the house before Rosie and Herb catch us."

As they left the grove of trees, he glanced at Damon and Finn. *Brothers.* He'd never had any, but now he did. That felt damned good.

1

"RINGO, THIS IS shaping up to be a disaster." Cade leaned down to give the gray tabby a good scratch. Ringo's motor started up, and the soothing purr lifted Cade's spirits, but not by much. Whenever he glanced at the glossy black horse peering at him over the stall door, anxiety curdled in his gut.

A couple of hours ago, his boss at the Circle T had vowed to sell Hematite to a meatpacking plant. Dick Thornwood was the kind of SOB who would do it, too, so Cade had driven into Colorado Springs and emptied his bank account. He had more in his pocket than Thornwood could get at a slaughterhouse, so logically Thornwood should sell the horse to him instead.

But logic wasn't his boss's strong suit, especially when his pride had been wounded. His decision to ride Hematite earlier that afternoon had been ill-advised, and to make matters worse, he'd chosen to do it with his new girlfriend watching. Cade had tried to talk him out of it, but he'd insisted. Hematite had tossed him in the dirt.

Just as Cade had predicted he would. They were mere days into the training program, and Hematite had major issues. He'd been mistreated as a colt and gelding him hadn't done much to settle him down. He'd just begun to trust Cade, who'd managed to saddle him for the first time today. Too bad Thornwood had seen that and decided to show off for his lady friend.

When he'd been dumped on his ass, she'd laughed. Thornwood had sent her packing, and then, shaking with rage, he'd approached the horse. Thank God he hadn't had a gun. Instead he'd delivered Hematite's death sentence before stomping up to the house.

Cade had been nervous about leaving for the bank, so he'd asked Douglas, the foreman, to keep an eye on Hematite. Fortunately nothing happened. Thornwood was likely up at the house drinking. Cade had brought fast food with him so he could stay in the barn and keep watch over the horse all night.

Footsteps on the wooden barn floor jacked up his heart rate, but it turned out to be Douglas coming back, probably to check on them.

"The way that feline dotes on you, anybody'd think your pockets were stuffed with catnip." Douglas nudged back his hat and leaned against Hematite's stall. "You should probably take him when you leave or he'll die of a broken heart."

"Who says I'm leaving?"

"I saw your face when Thornwood started to go for that horse. Looked to me like you wanted to kill him."

"The thought occurred to me, but then I decided he wasn't worth it." Cade worked his fingers over Ringo's arched back, and the cat purred louder. "But yeah, I figure my time here is about up. I just have to work out the logistics."

"That's why I came to talk to you. You can borrow my horse trailer."

Cade glanced up. "Really? You don't need it?"

Douglas shrugged. "Not until next spring. If you can get it back to me by April, that'll be fine."

"I'll have it back real quick. I called a buddy over at the Bar Z and he said they might be able to use another hand, at least for the summer. I'll head there once I get Thornwood to sell me this horse."

The foreman sighed. "I dunno. He's crazy."

"Thornwood or the horse?"

"Thornwood. The horse is just scared."

"Yeah. Hematite can't stay here. Even before today's incident, I thought Thornwood and Hematite were a bad combination."

"You got your stuff together?"

Cade nodded. "Figured once the shit hit the fan, I needed to be ready to go. I—" The sound of heavy, deliberate footsteps and the jingle of spurs made whatever he'd been about to say irrelevant. Heart pounding, he rose to his feet as Dick Thornwood came toward them. He held a coiled stock whip in one hand and a rope in the other. The fires of hell shone in his pale eyes.

Douglas swore under his breath, and Ringo crept behind a hay bale.

As Cade faced his boss, his heart rate slowed and icy calm replaced the initial adrenaline rush. He knew that unholy expression well. Bullies were all alike. His father, Rance, had looked exactly like that after he'd been drinking, except he'd vented his rage on Cade and his mother, not on a horse. Finally Cade had grown tall enough to stop him and his father had left.

Positioning himself in front of the stall door, Cade fixed his gaze on Thornwood. "I'll buy him from you."

Thornwood kept coming, bourbon on his breath. "He's not for sale."

"I thought you wanted him destroyed."

"I've reconsidered." He reached the stall. "Stand aside, Gallagher."

"No."

Thornwood's nostrils flared. "I *said* stand aside, cowboy!"

"No."

Dropping the rope, Thornwood uncoiled the whip. "Move it!"

"Touch me with that whip and I'll charge you with assault. And I have a witness."

Thornwood's jaw worked. "You're fired, asshole."

"Okay."

"And I'm not selling you that damned horse!"

"Why not?" He kept his tone conversational. "I'll give you more than you'd get at the slaughterhouse, and I'll take him off your hands. You can be rid of both of us tonight."

A vein pulsed at Thornwood's temple as his face reddened. "I'd rather beat the shit out of both of you." He sneered at Cade. "And your precious witness won't say a damned thing about it."

Cade raised his eyebrows. "You think he'd lie for you?"

"I do." Thornwood snapped the whip against the barn floor.

"I wouldn't count on it." Cade widened his stance.

"But if you're determined to pick a fight with me, bring it on." He held Thornwood's gaze. "Take your best shot."

A flicker in those pale eyes told Cade all he needed to know. Bullies chose fights they were certain they could win, and Thornwood was no longer so certain, even with that whip.

Sure enough, he backed up a step and his lip curled. "You're not worth the energy. Get the hell off my ranch. And take that nag with you." He pivoted toward the barn's entrance.

"Oh, no, you don't! You're selling him to me, not giving him away. I don't intend to get jailed for stealing your horse."

Thornwood paused but didn't turn around. "How much you got?"

Cade gave him a figure, everything he had in his pocket minus what he needed to carry him until he had another job.

"Give it to Lindstrom. He'll handle it." Thornwood stalked out of the barn.

Douglas blew out a breath. "Damn. That was close."

"He's just like my old man. Once you stand up to guys like that, they fold."

"Not always."

"No, not always." Cade had challenged his dad before he could back up the threat, and he had the scars to prove it. He dug the roll of bills out of his pocket. "I want something in writing that says I own this horse. Something with his signature on it."

"I'll see to it. You hitch up the trailer and get him loaded. I'll have a signed bill of sale for you before you leave."

"Thanks. I'll need to take the halter, too, and borrow a lead rope. Is that going to be a problem?"

"Nah. If he even brings it up, I'll tell him you'll return those when you return my trailer."

"I couldn't manage this without you." Cade gazed at the foreman. "I appreciate the help."

"Glad to do it."

"I won't be that far away. We can still get together for a beer once in a while."

"I'd like that." The foreman pocketed the money. "Better get moving before he changes his mind."

"Right. See you in a few." Cade fished for his keys and headed out the back to fetch his truck. He really was going to miss the crusty old foreman.

His reason for gravitating toward him in the first place was no mystery. He resembled Cade's foster father—about the same age with a similar wiry build and a no-nonsense attitude. Cade hadn't set foot on Thunder Mountain Ranch in... Damn, had it really been five years?

He talked to Herb and Rosie on the phone several times a year and always on Christmas Eve, but he'd avoided an actual visit because of Lexi. That was a chickenshit reason. He needed to man up and make the trip, although he couldn't expect vacation days for a while if he was about to start a new job.

Climbing into his truck, he drove behind the bunkhouse and hitched up Douglas's trailer. Then he took a moment to call his buddy at the Bar Z to make sure spending the night there was still an option. Tomorrow Cade would talk to the owner about a job, and with luck he'd be employed again in no time. That was important, especially when he had another mouth to feed.

Convincing Thornwood to sell had been the easy part of this rescue operation. Now he had to get that high-strung horse in the trailer. The previous owner, the one who'd mishandled Hematite's training, had given him a heavy-duty tranquilizer so he'd load. The drugged horse had staggered down the ramp the day he'd arrived.

This time Hematite would have to load and unload cold turkey. Cade considered that as he drove his truck around to the front of the barn. Lowering the ramp, he paused and took several deep breaths before going back into the barn.

His behavior would influence the horse, so the calmer he stayed, the better chance he'd have of keeping Hematite mellow. He visualized the horse walking quietly out of his stall, down the wooden aisle of the barn, then moving up into the trailer without hesitation.

Grabbing the rattiest-looking lead rope from the tack room, he started toward Hematite's stall. The horse watched him, ears pricked forward. Cade usually saved his next technique for when he was alone with a horse. Nobody else was in the barn, so he began singing "Red River Valley." Thanks to his time at Thunder Mountain Ranch, he had a whole repertoire of campfire songs, and normally they worked like a charm to settle nervous horses.

He'd only sung to Hematite a couple of times, though. They hadn't developed a singing routine, but at this point anything was worth a try. He continued the sweet love song as he unlatched the stall door and stepped inside.

Hematite snorted and edged away. Still singing, Cade approached and managed to clip the lead rope onto the horse's halter. Then he turned and walked out of the stall as if he thoroughly expected Hematite to follow him, no questions asked. The horse did.

Cade finished "Red River Valley" and moved on to "Tumbling Tumbleweeds." He sang in rhythm with the steady clip-clop of Hematite's hooves on the barn floor. Meanwhile he continued to visualize a smooth entrance into the horse trailer.

Out the barn door. Up the ramp. Cade kept singing. About three minutes later, the horse was loaded and the trailer doors secured. Cade stood there grinning and shaking his head in disbelief. That horse would be serenaded from now on.

"That's about the slickest thing I ever did see." Douglas came toward him from the direction of the house. "Were you *singing* to that animal?"

"Um, yeah." Cade chuckled. "If you use the term loosely."

"You're no George Strait, but at least I could recognize the tune. I've heard of using songs to calm a herd of cattle, but I never thought of trying it with horses. How long you been doing that?"

"Three or four years, I guess."

"No kidding. How'd you come up with it?"

"By accident. One day I was riding along, humming to myself for some reason, and I could feel my horse relax. So then I tried humming when I worked with a problem horse, and that seemed to help. I don't know if singing is any better than humming, but it's more interesting for me."

"I'll be damned." Douglas rubbed a hand over his jaw. "I'll just have to try it. Although I sound like a mating bullfrog, so it might not work for me. Can't believe

I've known you for almost two years and never realized you were a singing cowboy."

Cade laughed. "I wouldn't go that far."

"I would. You're a cowboy. You sing. Case closed. Oh, and here's your bill of sale, complete with Thornwood's signature. He's had enough to drink that he doesn't care about much of anything, so he was more than happy to sign."

"Thank you." Cade took the paper, opened it to check the signature and refolded it. "You have my cell number. If he gives you any grief about this after he sobers up, let me know."

"I doubt he will. I'll wager that by tomorrow he'll have rewritten history. He'll tell everyone he gave you the deal of a lifetime because he's such a great guy and he felt sorry for you."

"He can make up any story he wants as long as he leaves me and this horse alone."

"I think he will, but if I get any hint that he's on the warpath, I'll give you a holler."

"Thanks, Douglas." He shook the foreman's hand. "Don't forget. We're going to have that beer someday soon."

"I'm counting on it."

Climbing into the truck, Cade glanced around at the place he'd called home for eighteen months. It hadn't really been home, of course. Thunder Mountain was the only place that fit that description. Thornwood had been a lousy boss, but Douglas had made up for that. So it was with mixed feelings that Cade put the truck in gear and pulled away from the Circle T.

He'd made it to the main road by the time Ringo decided to show himself. The gray tabby crawled from the space behind the passenger seat and settled himself on the worn upholstery. Immediately he began to purr.

Cade sighed. He should probably turn around and take Ringo back to the Circle T. "Look, I'm heading over to a ranch that may have a territorial barn cat for all I know. You might not be welcome there. Then what?"

Ringo blinked at him and purred louder.

Cade's chest tightened. He'd never had a pet of his own. Dogs and cats had been a constant presence at Thunder Mountain Ranch, but they'd been loved and cared for by all the boys. Cade remembered each one fondly, but he'd never felt the deep connection that he'd formed with Ringo. Apparently Ringo returned the sentiment, because here he was ready to follow Cade wherever the road led.

"Okay, cat. We'll figure it out."

As if he understood that the matter was settled, Ringo curled up on the seat and closed his eyes.

That kind of trust was rare in this world. Cade hadn't experienced it often. He could count on one hand the people who trusted him like that—Herb, Rosie, Damon, Finn, Douglas. Not Lexi.

If Ringo was offering him that level of trust, he'd be a fool not to take it and be grateful. He'd also be very careful not to betray it. He knew what abandonment felt like, and he wouldn't wish that on any creature.

Lexi might think he'd abandoned her, but he'd been very careful not to make promises he couldn't keep. That's what he told himself whenever guilty memories of her anger and her tears plagued him. She'd had expectations he couldn't meet. According to Lexi, some things were just understood. Not in his world. He was a guy who spelled everything out, and he'd never, ever said he'd marry her.

The Bar Z was only a forty-five-minute drive from the Circle T. About halfway there, Cade's cell phone rang. He pulled it off its holder on the dash, expecting a call from his buddy or maybe from Douglas.

Instead he stared in disbelief at the name on the screen. Lexi Simmons. Damned spooky, as if she'd tuned in to his thoughts and picked up the phone.

But he didn't believe in mental telepathy, and he knew she wouldn't call because she'd magically tapped into his brain waves. He had a bad feeling that he wouldn't like what he was about to hear. Heart racing, he answered while looking for a place to pull over.

"Cade?" She sounded the same, and her musical voice hurt his heart in ways it hadn't hurt in years. "Can you talk?"

"In a minute." He sounded out of breath and hated that. But he *was* having trouble breathing. *Lexi. Dear God.* "I'm driving and hauling a horse behind me. Let me get off the road."

"Okay. I'll wait."

He set the phone back in its holder and eased to the shoulder so he wouldn't jostle Hematite. Then he grabbed the phone again. "I'm here. What's up?"

"It's Rosie. She… Herb took her to Sheridan Memorial."

He felt dizzy. "Why? What happened?"

"We won't know until they do some tests, so we shouldn't jump to conclusions, but—"

"Damn it, Lexi! What's wrong with her?"

"She might… She might have had a heart attack."

"No. Oh, no." Panic gripped him. "She can't. She's too young. She can't have a heart attack. She—"

"Maybe it's not that. But Herb's scared. He asked me to come and take care of things here."

"Did he ask you to call me?"

"No. I'm doing that on my own. I thought you should know."

"Damn right I should know! I'm a little north of Colorado Springs right now. I'll get there as soon as I can."

"Can you do that? Where were you going before I called?"

"It doesn't matter. I'm changing my plans."

"But you're hauling a horse."

"And the ranch has a barn."

"True." She hesitated. "So you're alone?"

"No."

"Oh."

He couldn't help smiling. He knew that tone. She hadn't liked his answer. "I have a cat."

"Oh!"

"Yeah, he came along for the ride. Are there any barn cats at the ranch?"

"Not right now."

"Dogs?"

"No, no dogs, either."

"That's just as well, then. Did you call Damon and Finn?"

"I don't have their numbers."

So she only had his. She'd kept it in her phone for five years. He shouldn't read too much into that, but he already was. "I'll call them. And if you hear anything more about Mom, call me. I'll see you in a few hours."

"Good. That's good." She hung up.

He wondered how she'd meant that and if she'd be glad to see him. The thought of seeing her made him nervous, but now that he had no choice in the matter, he discovered that he wanted to. His mental picture was five years old, so she'd probably look different.

Her hazel eyes would be the same, but guaranteed her hair would have changed. Women tended to do that, and she'd complained about her natural color. He liked the warm brown, but she might have dyed it or cut it.

When he'd talked to his foster mother on Christmas Eve, she'd said Lexi had broken up with her latest boyfriend. And now Rosie was in the hospital. How could he be thinking of Lexi and their screwed-up relationship when the mother of his heart was lying in a hospital bed?

First he called his buddy at the Bar Z to say he wouldn't be arriving, after all. Then he used the conference-call function on his phone to contact Damon and Finn. He didn't want to waste time repeating the news.

Eventually he got them both on the line. "Listen, I don't have time to talk, but Lexi called from the ranch and Mom's in the hospital with a possible heart attack. I'm driving up there now. I want both of you to get there as soon as you can arrange it."

"Absolutely," Damon said. "I'll text you once I have a plane ticket."

"Me, too." Finn sounded scared. "Is she gonna be okay?"

"Yes." Cade's jaw firmed. "She has to be."

2

LEXI DISCONNECTED THE PHONE, put on her denim jacket and walked straight out to the barn to prepare a stall for Cade's horse. Forking straw onto the floor and hay into the feed trough was the kind of physical labor she needed. Even so, she couldn't seem to stop shaking.

He'd sounded the same...but different. Older and maybe a little tired. She wondered where he'd been going with that horse at ten o'clock at night. And his cat.

Everything about the situation suggested that he'd been on the move, leaving one place to start afresh. Whatever his plans had been, he'd changed them immediately when he'd heard about Rosie, and that was gratifying. And endearing.

Knowing he was willing to drop everything to rush up here when the Padgetts needed him erased some of the resentment she'd felt over the years. He hadn't come back to visit them in so long. Damon and Finn had been back a few times, but they didn't have an ex-girlfriend they were trying to avoid. She'd heard mention of a reunion for all three of them, but that hadn't happened.

She'd lost track of how many boys had been fostered

at this ranch, but she guessed about two dozen, all told. The max at any one time had been eleven. In the last years of the program she'd given free riding lessons to any who'd wanted them. Since Rosie and Herb's retirement, several of the other guys had paid visits to the ranch, and she'd driven out to say hello and catch up on their lives.

But the three men who called themselves the Thunder Mountain Brotherhood were the ones Rosie and Herb cherished the most. Lexi heard it in their voices whenever the Padgetts talked about them. She could understand the extra love they gave to those three. Cade, Damon and Finn had lived at the ranch the longest, so they were the ones Lexi remembered most vividly, too. Especially the frustratingly stubborn and sexy Cade Gallagher.

He'd been the first kid Rosie had taken in, the one who'd started it all. Rosie had worked with Lexi's mom at the Department of Family Services in Sheridan, and when Rosie had decided to create a foster program at the ranch, Lexi's parents had volunteered to paint bedrooms and set up bunks.

Eventually the program had outgrown the main house, so Lexi's folks had helped build three log cabins and a washhouse for the older kids. Lexi had tagged along, and she'd become like a daughter to the Padgetts.

She'd just turned thirteen at the start of the program, about the same age as the boys. She'd considered them awkward and unappealing, not worth her time, until one day soon after she'd turned sixteen.

The image of seventeen-year-old Cade coming out of the barn on a hot summer day, his shirt hanging open and his hat shoved back, still had the power to stir her. He'd been laughing about some prank Damon had pulled, and the flash of his white teeth in his tanned face had been the most beautiful thing Lexi had ever seen.

From that day forward, she'd nursed a massive crush, but she'd pretended the same indifference she'd always shown him. He'd had girls hanging all over him at school, and she hadn't relished joining that crowd of groupies. She'd expected him to ask one of his giggling admirers to the prom.

Then, to her complete shock, he'd asked her. He'd even seemed nervous about it, as if expecting to be rejected. Heart pounding, she'd said yes, and in that instant, everything had changed. They'd become inseparable. High school had given way to community college, and exploratory touching had given way to hot, sweaty nights in the back of his pickup.

She'd assumed love, great sex and easy companionship would result in a proposal. She'd assumed wrong. Her lack of a ring had become a running joke among her friends, and she'd finally confronted him about their future.

They'd only had one big fight, but it had been a doozy. He'd learned that she expected marriage, and she'd learned he had no such ideas. He'd left town, and she'd cried into her pillow every night. Eventually her friends had staged an intervention and had set her up with somebody's cousin.

That had gone well enough that she'd started dating again. Although she was currently unattached, she'd had two serious boyfriends since Cade. She'd told herself that she'd moved on.

But if just hearing his voice on the phone had turned her into a quivering mess, she'd been kidding herself.

When he'd said he wasn't alone, she'd felt sick to her stomach at the thought of him bringing a woman back here. Discovering he was traveling with a cat instead had made her giddy with relief. She wasn't over Cade Gallagher, not by a long shot.

After putting away the pitchfork, she returned to the house and used her phone to look up the driving distance from Colorado Springs to Sheridan. Seven hours, give or take. That meant he'd show up before dawn. She had more than six hours to wait, and she should spend part of those sleeping. But that might be easier said than done.

She wandered through the house that she knew just as well as the one she'd grown up in. This rambling place with its five bedrooms, big kitchen with a rec room attached, comfy living room and wide front porch felt like home, too. Her little duplex in Sheridan was fine for now, but she dreamed of owning something like this eventually.

Maybe she'd play a little pool to wind down. The old table in the middle of the rec room had doubled as a dining table after the number of boys had topped out at eleven. A piece of thick plywood had been laid on top and folding chairs placed around it. In those days Rosie had hired a woman to help her cook, but the boys had been expected to clean up after themselves.

The balls were racked and the pool cues lined up. Maybe she wouldn't play, after all. It would only remind her of Cade, his green gaze intense as he focused on sending the eight ball into the pocket. Damon sometimes beat him, but nobody else stood a chance.

Turning out the overhead light, she walked back into the living room. She sat on the cushy sofa in front of the unlit fireplace and pulled off her boots. How empty the house felt without Herb and Rosie. They were supposed to be enjoying their well-deserved retirement, not sitting in the hospital worrying about whether Rosie had a serious health problem.

It wasn't fair, but getting to know the foster boys who'd stayed here had taught Lexi that life wasn't fair. Most of their stories were sad and quite often had left scars. She'd seen Cade's physical scars, but she hadn't given enough thought to his mental ones when she'd demanded a commitment.

An afghan Rosie had crocheted lay across the back of the sofa. Lexi pulled it over herself and snuggled down on one of the soft throw pillows. Whether or not Cade had changed in five years, she certainly had.

Back then she'd thought marriage to Cade was all she wanted in the world. Instead her career as a riding instructor had expanded beyond her wildest hopes. She still taught locally, but her reputation had spread and she'd been asked to give clinics all over the state.

If her business continued to grow, she could expect to have requests from other parts of the country. Marriage was the furthest thing from her mind these days. That was something to hold on to as she dealt with her feelings about Cade.

Although he could still throw her for a loop, she wasn't the needy woman he'd left. Yes, he'd been sex personified five years ago, but he could have changed, too. And with any luck, he'd grown fat.

Smiling at the thought of a pudgy Cade Gallagher, she drifted off to sleep. Of course she dreamed about being naked in his arms. They were making wild love that caused the headboard to bang against the wall.

Odd, because she'd never shared a bed with him, just the back of his pickup.

He called her name, and she… Hold on a minute. That wasn't a headboard banging against the wall. That was someone knocking on the front door. *Cade.*

"Lexi?" More knocking. "You in there?"

"Yeah!" She threw off the afghan and scrambled to her feet. "Coming!" Then she thought of her dream and giggled. The grandfather clock chimed four thirty. He'd made damned good time considering he'd been pulling a horse trailer.

Finger-combing her hair, she padded in her sock feet over to the door. Adrenaline pumped through her as she unlocked it. *Please let him be fat.* Her prayer went unanswered. Cade stood in the glow from the porch light looking lean and muscled. The stubble on his chin added to the image of a virile man in his prime.

Dark lashes framed the moss-green eyes she'd seen so often in her dreams. Concern shone there, and her heart lurched. He was still one hot cowboy, maybe even hotter than he'd been at twenty-three. Her body responded with embarrassing eagerness. She clenched the doorknob.

"Any more word?" He sounded exhausted.

"Uh, no." She cleared the huskiness from her throat. "Sorry."

He sighed. "Didn't think so. You said you'd call." He held her gaze as if looking for something in her expression.

If he hoped to find longing, it was probably there. Once upon a time, they'd found comfort in each other's arms. "You got here fast."

"Yeah." He took a step closer.

She held her breath. Would he pull her into his arms for a warm hug? Bad idea. A hug could easily become something more. Would he kiss her? Would she kiss him back?

With a low curse, he backed up again. "I should… get to the hospital."

"Right." *Good.* He was restraining himself. Better for both of them. "Just unhitch the trailer and go. I can take care of your horse."

He gave her a crooked grin. "I'm not so sure about that. How's your rendition of 'Red River Valley'?"

"Excuse me?" His grin sent her pulse racing again. No other man's smile had that effect on her.

"Never mind. Let's start with the cat. His name is Ringo."

"For the drummer?"

"No, for the outlaw from the Old West. He's a stowaway, so I don't have anything for him. No food, no litter box, nothing."

"I can rig up a temporary litter box. And I'll bet Rosie has cans of tuna in the pantry. She still makes that casserole with the potato chips."

"I loved that casserole. Haven't had it in five years."

"I'm sure she'll make it for you." Then reality hit her again. "I mean, after she comes home and…and feels better."

Cade's expression grew fierce. "She'll be home. And she'll feel better."

"Of course she will." She shared the underlying panic that made him glare at her that way. "They'll figure out the problem, and she'll be good as new."

"I'll get Ringo." And the brawny cowboy left the porch to fetch his cat.

Lexi found that sweet, even more touching than if he'd arrived with a dog. Guys were supposed to love dogs, but it took a secure man to bond with a cat. Obviously she was still hooked on Cade. All he had to do was show up looking adorably rumpled with a cat in tow and she was ready to hurl herself into his arms. She'd have to be careful.

He came back cradling a gray tabby. "He's used to staying in the barn, but I'm afraid if I leave him out there and take off, he'll run away. He mostly wants to be wherever I am, so he might come looking for me."

Lexi wasn't surprised. Cade had always been a magnet for animals—and people. She was only one of many who'd longed to be close to this warmhearted but complicated man. As she stepped back from the open door to let Cade walk in, Ringo eyed her as if suspecting she had plans to separate him from the person he adored.

She had enough experience with cats to know that releasing Ringo into a large house where he could find all sorts of hidey-holes was a bad idea. "Let me open a can of tuna, and then we'll take him into the guest bath so he'll be contained in one spot. The tuna might distract him enough for you to slip out of here without too much fuss."

"Good idea."

"I'll be right back." She started toward the kitchen.

"You look great, by the way."

She glanced over her shoulder to find him watching her with warmth in his green eyes. "Thanks. You, too." Her heart beat faster as she hurried into the kitchen. She knew that look far too well. It had gotten her into a lot of trouble in the past. She didn't need that kind of trouble now.

Rosie's pantry was neatly organized, which made the tuna easy to find. As Lexi carried it over to the electric can opener sitting on the counter, she heard Cade murmuring to the cat. The soft rumble of his voice stirred more hot memories, damn it. She shoved the tuna under the can opener's blade so the sharp buzz of the motor could drown him out. She'd seriously underestimated his ability to arouse her just by being Cade.

Then his murmurs turned to a surprised "Hey!" A second later Ringo wound his furry body through her legs, his plaintive meow announcing that he'd smelled the tuna.

"Sorry about that." Cade appeared in the kitchen. "I didn't anticipate his leap for freedom. He's probably really hungry."

"How about you?"

"I'm fine. I'll get something after I see Mom."

"Okay." Lexi tamped down the urge to offer a sandwich for the road. She didn't need to leap into her former role of nurturing girlfriend. He was a grown man who'd managed to take care of himself without her help for the past five years.

Instead she opened a cupboard, took out a shallow bowl and dumped the tuna into it. "I'll bet if I carry this into the bathroom, he'll follow me. You might as well go unload your horse and save some time."

"Hang on—let me see if Mom has carrots." He opened the refrigerator door and rummaged in the vegetable bin with the ease of someone who'd done it thousands of times. "Perfect. I'm outta here." He edged the door closed with his hip and backed out of the kitchen while keeping his attention on the cat. Ringo stayed right by Lexi's feet and continued his frantic meowing.

Once Lexi heard the front door shut, she walked down the hallway and into the guest bath with Ringo in hot pursuit. She set the bowl on the tile, and he buried his nose in it. Quietly she backed out and closed the bathroom door. Later she'd find something to use as a litter box.

After putting on her boots and jacket, she stepped outside in time to see a large black horse backing slowly down the trailer ramp. Cade had a gentle grip on the lead rope. And he was singing.

He had a decent voice, one of the few things about him she'd forgotten over the years. She remembered it now as she listened to his rendition of "Red River Valley." The kids had sung it around the campfire at Thunder Mountain. Back then she'd joined the others in making fun of the sentimental words, but tonight they made her heart ache.

Cade completed the maneuver and paused at the bottom of the ramp to reward the horse with a piece of carrot. Apparently a sound track helped the animal behave. Her career had brought her in contact with a riding instructor who encouraged her students to hum or sing when they were nervous. Lexi had adopted the technique for calming uneasy riders, but she hadn't considered using it for the horses. Now she would.

She waited until Cade finished his song before she left the porch and walked slowly over to him. The horse's coat gleamed in the dusk-to-dawn spotlights that illuminated the circular drive. "He's a beauty, Cade."

"I had to buy him so I could get him away from my former boss. If he'd stayed there, he would have ended up dead sooner or later."

Lexi shuddered. "Then I'm glad you bought him. What's his name?" She approached with care.

"Hematite. He was abused as a colt, dismissed as a discipline problem by the time he was two and sold cheap to my boss less than a month ago. Thornwood expected me to straighten him out."

"Looks as if you're making progress. He unloaded well."

"And I'm damned glad he did. There were no guarantees."

"It's dumb to make guarantees where horses are concerned." Lexi surveyed Hematite. "But as of now, he seems docile enough. Want me to take it from here? I know you're eager to get to the hospital."

"I am, but I think it would be best if I lead him into the barn. Just let me know where to put him."

"Follow me." She wasn't about to push it. Cade knew his horse, and she didn't relish the thought of dealing with an unpredictable animal tonight. Swinging open the double barn doors, she turned on the lights along the aisle between the rows of stalls. "Second one on the right. I laid down fresh straw and put a flake of hay in the feeder. Water's turned on, too." She walked ahead of him and opened the stall door.

"Thanks. This is great." He led Hematite into the stall, unhooked the lead rope and rubbed the horse's neck. "You're safe now, buddy. I'll be back to check on you in a few hours."

Hematite bumped his nose against Cade's arm. Then he walked over to the hay rack and began to munch.

Cade let out a breath as he left the stall and latched it behind him. While he coiled the lead rope, he gazed at the horse. "If I didn't know better, I'd think he understood what I just told him. I've never seen him so relaxed."

"At the very least, he probably picked up on your relief."

"I *am* relieved. I had no idea if this would work, if I could transport him from hell to heaven." He glanced at Lexi. "Thanks for making it possible."

She shrugged. "Don't thank me. I'm only doing what Herb and Rosie would have wanted."

"I appreciate it, all the same." He looked around the barn as if noticing his surroundings for the first time. "Wait, why are there three other horses in here? I thought they were only planning to keep Navarre and Isabeau."

"I have the same question. The last time I came out to see them, they only had those two, but that was a couple of months ago. When Herb called tonight, he wasn't all that coherent, but I gathered they're boarding."

Cade frowned. "Boarding? Why?"

"You'll have to ask him. I have no clue unless they need something more to take care of. That would fit."

He repositioned his hat in a typical Cade gesture. "I suppose so. They love to be of service, thank God. If they hadn't come along…"

Her heart squeezed. "I know."

"Yes, you do." He held her gaze. "You know that more than anyone. Lexi, I—"

"Go see Rosie." She wasn't ready for a heart-to-heart. "We're both tired. We'll talk later."

He nodded. "All right. But let me say this much. I've missed you every single day."

She swallowed her instinctive response. She'd missed

him every single day, too, but she wasn't going to admit it. "Go see Rosie."

He turned as if to walk out of the barn. Then he swung back and reached for her. Before she could protest he'd pulled her into his arms and brought his mouth down on hers. It was a hard kiss, a kiss filled with frustration. There was no tenderness, only heat and confusion. It was over before she could respond.

He left the barn without looking back. Heart pounding, she pressed her fingers to her mouth. She still loved him with every fiber of her being. And he still loved her. But as she'd learned five years ago, love wasn't enough.

3

CADE WASN'T A fan of hospitals, especially this one. His mother had died here when he was barely thirteen, before he'd had a firm grasp on the concept of cancer. Years later he'd concluded that the actual cause of death had been hopelessness. But that wasn't a medical term, so cancer had been listed instead.

Coming back here took some white-knuckled determination on his part, but Rosie lay in one of these rooms, so that meant he had to slay his dragons. Everyone he met on his way to her room was wonderful. It wasn't their fault that he dreaded walking these halls with his mother's ghost at his side.

When he came into the room, the sight was terrifyingly familiar. Rosie appeared to be asleep in that sterile white bed, and she was hooked up to a bunch of monitors. Herb rose from a chair and came over to enfold him in a fierce, silent hug. The guy was more bony and fragile than Cade remembered.

For the first time he realized that these people who had been the seawall standing between him and drowning were now vulnerable and in need of protection. That thought focused him more than any other. He could do this.

Herb released him and motioned for them to go into the hall. "She's finally asleep," he murmured. "I'd hate to wake her up, although she'll be excited to see you. Did Lexi call you?"

"She did."

Herb nodded. "Not surprised. She's good that way. You sure didn't waste any time getting here."

"I started out right after she called."

"Your boss is okay with you taking time off?"

"I quit." Technically he'd been fired, but better not to get into the full story right now.

"Not because of this, I hope."

"No, no. I was headed over to another possible job when Lexi called. It's fine, Dad. I can stay as long as you need me."

Emotion welled in Herb's gray eyes, and he glanced away in obvious embarrassment. "That's…that's mighty nice to hear. But we'll be okay." He cleared his throat and bravely met Cade's gaze. "Just a little bump in the road."

"Of course it is. I never thought anything different. But since I was between jobs, I figured I'd come on up for a visit."

"I'm real glad you did. It's good to see you, son." He turned back toward the room where Rosie continued to sleep. "I should get back in there. I don't like leaving her alone in case one of those monitors does something funky. But if you drove all night, you must need food or at least a cup of coffee."

"Just coffee. Can I bring you some?"

"Sure. That'd be great." He reached in his hip pocket for his wallet.

"Put your money away. Coffee's on me. But listen, I wanted to ask something."

"What's that?"

"What are those three extra horses doing in the barn?"

Herb looked startled. "How do you know about that?"

"I have a horse now, and I had to drop him off when I got to Thunder Mountain."

"Oh." Herb rubbed the gray stubble on his chin. He was only five years older than when Cade had seen him last, but he appeared to have aged considerably more than that. "Rosie and I figured we shouldn't let the space sit idle."

Cade smiled. "Getting a little bored maybe?"

"I guess you could say that."

"Just wondered. I'll get us some coffee. Be back in a flash." Moments later, he located a coffee machine in the waiting room, and, as the first cup began to fill, he blew out a breath. So far he'd held himself together, but he could use backup. Good thing he'd called Damon and Finn.

That reminded him to check his phone. Sure enough, he had a text from Damon. He'd be landing at the Sheridan airport around one and wondered if he should rent a car. While the second cup of coffee filled, Cade replied that he'd pick him up.

Immediately Damon texted back.

How's Mom?

Sleeping.

It wasn't much, but it was all Cade knew. He felt a rush of gratitude for Damon, who obviously was worried, too. Having him here, along with Finn, would mean a lot to Rosie and Herb but also to Cade.

By the time he returned with the coffee, Herb was outside the room talking to a fiftyish brunette. A couple of nurses bustled around in Rosie's room, and the curtains had been drawn around her bed. The brunette hadn't noticed him yet, so Cade paused to get his bearings. *Yep. Janine Simmons, Lexi's mom.*

Then Herb glanced his way. "Here's Cade. The nurses kicked us out, son. Taking vital signs and such."

Janine looked as if she'd rushed over without putting on makeup or fixing her hair. She had Lexi's eyes, something that had always made her seem accessible and familiar. But there was nothing friendly about her expression now. "Hello, Cade."

"Good to see you again, Mrs. Simmons." He handed one of the cups to his dad and offered her the other one. "You're welcome to this if you want it." As a peace offering it wasn't much. Five years ago he'd broken her daughter's heart. A cup of coffee from a vending machine probably didn't make up for that.

"Thanks, but I need to get going. Lexi called me a little while ago to tell me Rosie was in the hospital, so I threw on some clothes and came over. Aaron's at a dental conference in Billings so I have to go home and feed the dogs." She gave Herb a quick hug. "I'll be back in a couple of hours. Call if you need anything in the meantime."

"Thanks, Janine. I will."

Her gaze flicked to Cade. "It's good that you're here."

"I know." He accepted the rebuke in her voice. He deserved it for…many reasons.

As she walked away, Herb put a hand on Cade's shoulder. "Don't let her lay a guilt trip on you."

"But I *am* guilty. First I disappointed her daughter, and then I let my issues with Lexi keep me from coming to see you and Mom."

"Water under the bridge. You're here now, and that's all that counts. No point in dwelling on the past unless you're remembering good stuff."

Cade absorbed the wisdom of that. "I've really missed you." He hadn't realized how much.

"I missed you, too, but I don't ever want you or any of the boys to feel obligated to come and see us. That's not how we roll." He took a sip of the coffee and grimaced.

"Sorry. It's what I could find."

"Never mind. You're supposed to get bad coffee in these situations. I think it's a rule."

Cade smiled, relieved to see some of Herb's spunk returning. He drank his coffee, and sure enough, it was awful. "By the way, I heard from Damon. I'll pick him up from the airport at one this afternoon."

Herb's bushy eyebrows rose. "Lexi called him, too?"

"No, I did." He sipped the coffee because he needed the caffeine. "Finn, too."

"You're starting to scare me, boy. Rosie's not about to die, you know. It could be nothing more than indigestion."

If Cade hadn't experienced the desperate hug when he'd first walked in, he might have believed Herb wasn't concerned. But the little speech was pure bravado.

Cade wasn't going to call him on it, though. "I realize that. We're all just looking for a good excuse to pester you guys."

"Cade?" Rosie's voice caused them both to turn toward the open door. "Is that you out there?"

"Yes, ma'am."

Rosie made an impatient noise and addressed the nurses who were still in the room. "Hey, you two, I'd surely appreciate it if you could put me back to rights and open the curtains. I need to hug my son."

Both of them laughed. "Rosie, are you going to be a difficult patient?" one asked.

"Only if this blood-pressure business takes all blessed morning, Sally."

More laughter and teasing followed. Cade should have anticipated that Rosie would be on a first-name basis with the hospital staff. She'd had a long career in social services and knew nearly everyone in town.

Eventually the curtain was pulled back, and both nurses headed for the door. The short, stocky one smiled at Cade as she came out of the room. "She's all yours, cowboy."

"And tell her to stop scaring us like that," said the taller one.

"Yes, ma'am." Cade polished off his coffee and looked around for a trash can.

"Cade?" Rosie sounded pretty strong for a sick woman. "Get a move on, son!"

"Give me that." Herb lifted the empty cup from his hand. "You go on in."

Cade took off his hat and made sure he had a smile on his face as he walked into the room. "You've been instructed to—"

"Yeah, yeah, I heard." Rosie looked a little pale, and her hair, which she'd started coloring a light blond, wasn't styled the way she normally did it. But her blue eyes were bright and filled with love. "Come over here, you big galoot."

His breathing stalled. She was so important to him. Herb was right that guilt didn't do anyone any good, so he'd work on eliminating that. But he might not be able to erase the regret over staying away so long.

Being careful of the IV, he leaned down and gave her a cautious hug. He breathed in the antiseptic smell that reminded him of bad times, but Rosie's signature floral scent was there, too, which he associated with good times. "I love you, Mom."

"I love you, too, but I hope you didn't jeopardize your job to come see me."

"Nope." He kissed her cheek and moved back. "Your timing was perfect."

"Glad to be so accommodating, but why was it perfect?"

"He quit last night," Herb said as he walked into the room. "I think there's a story there considering that he brought a horse with him."

"And a cat. I hadn't planned on the cat."

Rosie smiled. "It's like old times when you boys used to haul home every stray for miles around. So where are these animals now?"

"At the ranch. Lexi's watching them for me."

Speculation filled Rosie's gaze. "So you've talked to her, then."

"Yes, ma'am." He wondered if she could tell by his expression that he'd also kissed Lexi. Whenever he wasn't worrying about Rosie and what might be wrong with her, he was thinking about Lexi. He'd forgotten how good her mouth felt, and now he wanted to kiss her some more.

"How'd that go?"

"Fine." This wasn't the conversational direction he favored. "But enough about that. I want to know about you."

"You wouldn't be trying to change the subject, would you?" She gave him a knowing smile.

"Maybe. But seriously, what do the doctors think is going on?"

"They aren't sure yet, although I'll bet it's just a bad case of indigestion." Rosie's jaw firmed as if she wouldn't tolerate any other diagnosis.

"They have to run more tests," Herb said. "We should know something in another day or so. Like she says, it's probably nothing, but better to be safe than sorry."

Cade nodded. "Agreed."

"Anyway," Rosie said, "you can see I'm in good hands. Judging from the way you look, I'll bet you drove all night to get here. I appreciate you doing that, but now you should go back to the ranch and get some sleep."

"I'm okay."

"You're dead on your feet. Herb, talk him into going home. In fact, you should go with him. I'll be fine here."

Herb glanced at Cade. "I'm going to hang around a little longer, but she's right. Go home and rest. You can come back later, after you pick up Damon."

"After he does what?" Rosie pushed a button that adjusted the bed, letting her sit up a little more. "Damon's coming in?"

"At one today." Belatedly Cade realized that having them all descend might be alarming rather than comforting. "And Finn's coming, too, but that doesn't mean we think—"

"That I'm about to croak? I hope not! Unless Herb knows something he's not telling me."

"I swear I don't." Herb held up both hands. "I had nothing to do with this. Lexi called Cade, and Cade called the other two."

"And it might boil down to indigestion," Rosie repeated, shaking her head. "What in heaven's name did Lexi say to you, Cade, that started this frantic race to my bedside?"

"It's my fault." Herb scrubbed a hand over his face. "You showed all the classic signs of a heart attack. For all we know, you actually had one. When I called Lexi and asked her to come over and watch the place for us, I might have been a little…upset."

"Oh." Rosie's expression softened as she looked at her husband. "I guess I scared you worse than I thought."

Herb shrugged. "I, um…" He paused to clear his throat. "Yeah, I was scared."

Her voice was gentle. "You still are."

"A little. But you're looking lots better, and I'm sure you're right that it's nothing to be concerned about. Anyway, the boys will be here. That's good news, right?"

"Yes, it certainly is." Rosie glanced at Cade. "But when you talk to them, could you let them know I'm not at death's door? And don't let them bring flowers. That would really freak me out, if I thought I'd be in here long enough to need flowers."

"Got it." Cade hadn't thought about flowers, mostly because nothing had been open when he'd driven into town, but Damon and Finn might have insisted they bring her some. Good thing Rosie had said something or she likely would have ended up with three monster bouquets.

About that time his cell chimed, indicating a text. "That could be Finn." He pulled out his cell. "Yep. He'll be in a little after three."

Rosie sighed. "I don't want to think about what those plane tickets must have cost, but what's done is done, and I'll be tickled to see you all together again."

"I'm sure they don't care what the tickets cost." Just like Cade hadn't worried about giving up a potential job opportunity. Some things were more important.

"No, they probably don't care." Rosie gave him a fond smile. "That's the kind of guys you all are. I suppose you'll want to stay in your old cabin, but the beds aren't made and the place hasn't been dusted in months."

"Doesn't matter." Cade had assumed that's where they'd bunk. "Do you still keep the sheets and blankets in that big hall closet?"

"Yes, but if you all just sleep in the house, it'll mean less work for you."

"But it wouldn't be as much fun."

"I suppose not." She gazed at him. "Maybe Lexi would be willing to help you get that cabin ready."

"Nah, I can handle it." He wasn't sure how to approach the situation with Lexi, but he didn't want to start out by asking her to do chores that were rightly his.

"Go on home, Cade." Rosie made a shooing motion with her hand. "You have things to take care of."

"Okay." He gave her another peck on the cheek and left the room. Yes, he had several things to take care of, including his broken relationship with Lexi. When he'd been hundreds of miles away, he'd convinced himself to let her go. But that kiss had changed everything.

4

LEXI HAD SHOWERED and changed clothes by the time Cade's truck pulled up outside. Her frequent trips out of town for riding clinics had turned her into a speed packer, so when Herb had called to ask if she'd house-sit, she'd only needed five minutes to pack a bag before heading for Thunder Mountain Ranch.

Thank goodness she hadn't been on a trip when Herb had called. Her next gig was more than a week away, and by then— But she didn't really want to project too far ahead. Despite hearing from her mother that the situation seemed to be under control, Lexi couldn't erase the memory of Herb's frantic phone call.

He was an animal vet, not a people doctor, but if Herb had been scared, Lexi figured there'd been a reason. She was eager to hear Cade's opinion now that he'd actually seen Rosie. But that wasn't why her heart hammered and her breathing pattern changed when she heard his boots on the porch as he crossed to the front door.

It was unlocked because Herb and Rosie never bothered locking up during the day when they were home.

Although at one time Cade had enjoyed the freedom to walk right in, Lexi didn't think he'd assume that he could do it now. Rather than wait for his knock, she crossed to the door and opened it.

He looked even sexier than he had earlier. Or maybe that hard, desperate kiss had affected how she viewed him. His day's growth of beard was unusual, or it had been five years ago. He'd always said he kept his chin silky-smooth for her.

The prickle of his beard this morning had startled her because she wasn't used to that with Cade. But his lips had felt achingly familiar. Beard or no beard, she wanted to kiss him again.

He walked through the door and set down a battered duffel bag. "Thought I might as well bring this in so I can shave and shower at some point."

"Good idea." Her brisk tone covered a zing of aware-ness. It had been a natural thing for him to say, yet now she was thinking of stroking his freshly shaven cheek and breathing in the scent of soap. "How's Rosie?"

"Feisty."

"Yeah?" That surprised a chuckle out of her. "How so?"

He walked over to the couch and sank down on it. "She let me know that if I'd called the Brotherhood to-gether because I thought she was going to croak, that I'd seriously miscalculated. And she *really* doesn't want any of us bringing her flowers, FYI."

"That's funny." Lexi chose an easy chair that was at a right angle to the couch. "Any word from her doctors?"

He shook his head. "You know how that goes. They'll want to run a bunch of tests before they say anything definitive. Mom's convinced herself it's a false alarm, but..."

"You aren't so sure?"

He took off his hat and propped it on his knee. "No." Leaning his head against the back of the couch, he closed his eyes. "I want to be convinced, but when I first got there and hugged Dad, I could feel his fear. And he has a medical background, so it's not like he's clueless about what's going on."

"I thought the same thing." The way Cade leaned back and closed his eyes made her wonder if he had a headache. He used to get them when he was stressed. Having her massage his temples used to help, but the only surefire cure had been a round of hot sex.

"Anyway, they sent me home to get some sleep, but there's no time."

"Why not?"

He sat up and glanced at her. "Too many things to handle. By the way, I noticed you'd turned the horses out and put Hematite in the little paddock."

"I thought you'd want him isolated at first."

"You did exactly right. We need to see how he settles in here before turning him out with the others. But did he behave himself?"

"Sure did."

"Great. That's great. How about Ringo?"

"He's fine. I found a litter box in the storage shed along with half a bag of litter and a cat bed. You know Rosie and Herb, always figuring another stray will show up."

"Thanks for taking care of him for me. Damn. I should have stopped for cat food. I'll get some when I go back. He usually sleeps during the day, so I might as well leave him in the bathroom until I get the cabin ready."

She should have guessed he'd want to bunk there. "Have you heard from the guys?"

"I'm picking up Damon at one and Finn at three."

She checked the grandfather clock ticking away in the corner. "That gives you time to take a nap in one of the guest rooms. I'll get the cabin ready." He did have a headache, poor guy. She could see it in his eyes.

"Thanks, but I wouldn't feel right about that. My brothers, my job." He put on his hat and stood. "Mom said the sheets were still in the hall closet."

"They are, but I can do it." She followed him out of the living room.

"Not as well as I can. I'll bet you wouldn't think to stick a rubber snake in Finn's bed."

"Please tell me you're not going to do that."

He glanced at her and grinned.

"This isn't the time or place. Don't be an idiot."

"Too late." He chuckled as he opened the bifold doors and pulled sheets and pillowcases from a shelf labeled Bunk Beds.

"Cade!"

"I'm not going to do it, but it's good to know I can still get you riled up. Hold these while I pull out the blankets."

"And then you'll let me finish the job while you take a nap, right?"

"Wrong."

"What if you fall asleep at the wheel because you're exhausted?" She was caretaking, but she couldn't help it. If he pushed himself too far and something happened to him or the other two, then where would they be? The thought was unacceptable on so many levels, especially the deepest one, where Cade would live forever in her heart.

"I won't fall asleep at the wheel." After hauling blankets out of the closet, he folded them over his arm.

"Right. I keep forgetting that you're Superman."

"I keep forgetting that you have a smart mouth." He closed the closet doors and turned to her. "I'll take the sheets now."

She held on to them and stepped back. "Look, I don't want to tell you how to do this, but—"

"But you're about to."

"It's just that the cabin should be vacuumed before you take these out there or they'll get all dusty."

He paused. "Damn. You're right. Okay, we'll just pile this stuff on the couch until I'm ready for it. I wasn't thinking."

"Which is why—"

"Don't start with me." He glared at her as he walked back into the living room. "I'll be fine as long as I keep moving. Where's the vacuum cleaner?"

"You have a headache."

He laid the blankets on the couch. "You don't know that."

"Yes, I do. You have that squinty look." She deposited the sheets on top of the blankets. "You should at least lie down for a while."

He turned to her with a sigh. "Let up on me, okay? I'm doing the best I can with a shitty situation."

Remorse hit her. She'd allowed fear for his safety to turn her into a nagging pest, which wasn't getting either of them anywhere. "I'm sorry. I just—"

"I know." His voice gentled. "And you're right about

everything. I'm sure you'd be more efficient at getting the cabin ready. I should accept your generous offer and get some sleep. But I doubt I *could* sleep. I'm way too keyed up about Mom, and—" he paused "—about you."

She met his gaze. This might not be the time, but they wouldn't be alone like this much longer. "Would you ever have come back?"

"I don't know." He hesitated. "But I'm here now, and it's like I never left. No, that's not right. I want you as much as ever, even when you're a pain in the ass. I think I want you even more than I did before, but what used to be simple…isn't."

The heat in his eyes made her tremble. "It was never simple."

"Oh, sometimes it was. On a hot summer night when nothing mattered but taking off our clothes and losing ourselves in each other, it seemed pretty damned simple."

She was stunned into speechlessness. That brief, honest description hurled her back to those nights, and she ached for him as fiercely as she had then. In his mind, the sex had been fun and uncomplicated. She'd been the one who'd loaded down the relationship with expectations.

He blew out a breath. "But obviously that's not how you remember it. Let's postpone this discussion, okay? Just point me in the direction of the vacuum cleaner so I can get started."

She should do that and go about her business. But there he stood, so jacked up with worry and sexual frustration that he couldn't get the sleep he needed. She was pretty tense, too, but the few hours of rest she'd had meant her brain wasn't completely fried. "I have an idea."

"What's that?"

"We'll fix up the cabin together, so it'll go twice as fast. Then you don't have to feel guilty about me doing it while you're lying in a guest room staring at the ceiling."

He looked unsure, but at last he nodded. "I guess that'll be okay."

"I'll get the vacuum cleaner and a laundry basket so we can carry everything at once. Oh, and you'll need towels and washcloths, so pull some of those out of the closet. And bars of soap."

"Yeah, I forgot about that stuff." He rubbed a hand over his jaw. "I need to shower and get rid of this scruff before I go to the airport, or they'll think I've turned into a vagrant."

"Then you might as well bring your duffel, too."

"Makes sense."

Wow, that part had been easy. Her plan could still fall apart at any point along the way, and if it did, oh, well. But so far, so good. Anticipation and a slight case of nerves made her shiver as she headed for the laundry room where Rosie kept her canister vacuum cleaner.

Moments later they left the house with Cade lugging an oversize laundry basket full of linens and the vacuum. Lexi carried his duffel. Too bad she didn't have X-ray vision so she could see what was inside. When they'd been dating he'd always carried condoms, but that didn't mean he had any with him now.

He paused to gaze at the rugged Bighorn range, still dusted with snow above the tree line. "I've missed those mountains."

"So you didn't get attached to the ones in Colorado?"

"Oh, they're pretty enough, but these feel like home."

It was on the tip of her tongue to ask if that meant he might be moving back. But that was a loaded question. Instead, she resorted to a weather comment, always a safe topic. "It's a beautiful day."

He glanced up at the blue sky dotted here and there with white puffy clouds. "It is. Good weather seems weird when you have a crisis. Seems like it ought to be raining."

"I'm glad it's not, with sleepy people driving around."

"I know you're worried about that, but don't be." He started off toward the cabins again. "I'll be okay from here to the airport, and I can always put Damon behind the wheel once he gets here."

"You should definitely do that." She fell into step beside him. "Unless he's been up all night, too. Maybe I should drive you."

"No. Much as I appreciate the offer, I'm not being chauffeured to the airport to pick up my bro. That would be lame."

"Okay." She doubted he'd ask Damon to drive, either, but at least having a passenger should help keep him alert. Cade liked to think he didn't need any help, ever. That had been part of the problem when she'd been focused on wringing a commitment out of him.

They approached three tidy log cabins grouped in a partial semicircle in a meadow about thirty yards from the main house. In the center a ring of wooden benches surrounded a fire pit that had seen many cookouts. A shared washhouse behind the cabins had kept the plumbing costs down, although Lexi hadn't envied those boys having to go out there in the winter. But all the boys had acted as if trudging through the snow to wash up had been a test of their manhood.

"Sure brings back memories." Cade paused again to look around. "It's too quiet, though."

"I know what you mean." She fished the key out of her pocket and walked over to the first cabin in the row, the one Cade, Damon and Finn had claimed soon after it had been built. "I asked Herb and Rosie if they'd ever thought of renting these so they wouldn't sit empty, but they didn't seem interested."

"They might reconsider. Apparently they took in those other horses because they hated to see the stalls unused."

"So do you think they're finding retirement too tame?"

"Could be."

"Knowing them, that's not so surprising." She left his duffel outside and opened the door. The air was a little musty but not bad. The amenities consisted of two sets of bunk beds, four built-in desks, each with a lamp, two dressers and one closet. Cowboy-themed curtains hung at each of the four windows, but otherwise the room had no decorations.

Lexi opened a window and let in some fresh air. The last time she'd been in here, a couple of weeks before she and Cade had had their epic fight, the walls had been covered with posters, framed photographs and a nonworking neon Budweiser sign Finn had found at a yard sale.

The Thunder Mountain Brotherhood, as they'd dubbed themselves, had stayed on at the ranch after graduating from high school. They'd realized how much Herb and Rosie needed them to work with the younger kids. Cade had taken courses in equine behavior at Sheridan's community college, while Damon had apprenticed with a local carpenter and Finn had enrolled in online business classes until he was old enough to train as a bartender. But most of their free time had been devoted to helping Rosie and Herb.

Cade left the basket of linens on the front stoop next to his duffel and brought in the vacuum cleaner. "It's a little stark, isn't it?"

"Well, nobody's lived here for years."

Cade gazed around at the bare walls. "Even though I knew it would be like this, I somehow expected to come in and find everything the way it used to be."

"I could loan you a couple of my Remington prints for the time you're here."

He smiled at that. "Thanks, but we'll survive without art on the walls." He turned and reached up over the door to the beam above it. "This is still here. That's good." He traced the logo they'd created and carved into the wood. A stylized *TMB* was tucked under the outline of a jagged mountain peak.

"It's not as if Herb and Rosie would ever sand it off. I'm sure they love knowing it's there."

"They probably do." Cade stepped back and gazed up at the logo. Then he turned around. "I'm a jerk— you know that?"

"There have been times I would have agreed with you, but this isn't one of them."

"No, seriously. Just because I got spooked by the idea of tying myself down, I pulled away from all the important people in my life."

"While I'm flattered if you put me in that category—"

"I do."

"That's nice to hear, but even if you'd stayed, Damon and Finn would have left. You were the first to go, but Damon always intended to go to California for the real estate opportunities, and Finn's research told him Seattle was his best bet for the microbrewery."

"Once again, you're right." He shook his head. "God knows I should have learned that nothing stays the same."

"Some things do." *Like my love for you.* She wouldn't drop that bombshell now. She might never drop it. He was tired, and his emotions were frayed. Tomorrow he might not be nearly as susceptible to the nostalgia swamping him today.

"Like what?"

"Dust." She glanced at the vacuum cleaner in his hand. "Ready to activate that bad boy?"

"Absolutely. What's the plan?"

Somehow she kept from smiling. If he only knew. "I like to vacuum top to bottom, so if you start with your bunk, I can come behind you and put on the sheets while you vacuum Damon and Finn's bunks. I'll make up those while you take care of the other surfaces, and then we'll finish with the floor."

"Excellent." He walked over to his bunk. "Should I mess with the top part since nobody will be up there?"

"I'd say give it a once-over, so dust doesn't filter down on you."

"Good thinking. I'm on it." He located a plug and fired up the vacuum cleaner.

She allowed herself a moment to watch his back muscles flexing under his Western shirt as he wielded the vacuum. A video would go viral in seconds, especially if it included the part where he leaned over to reach the far corner of the bottom bunk and stretched the denim covering his mighty fine ass.

Damn, but he looked good. Five years had only added to his considerable sex appeal. He'd had girlfriends—of course he had—but she didn't want to think about him getting naked with anyone else.

"Are you ogling me?" he asked as he continued to work. Laughter rippled in his voice.

"Absolutely not." She spun around and stepped outside where they'd left the laundry basket full of linens.

"I do believe you were, Lexi Ann," he called over the noise of the vacuum.

"That's because you're so full of yourself," she called back as she fanned herself. *Whew.* She'd have to concentrate on her bed-making task or she was liable to jump him before they finished cleaning the place.

And they did need to finish, because he felt responsible for doing it. If her plan worked, she'd leave him sleeping like a baby in a nice clean cabin that was ready for his buddies. She'd wake him in time to get dressed and drive to the airport.

His voice rose over the whine of the vacuum. "My bunk's ready for you!"

Laughing, she scooped a set of sheets and a blanket out of the laundry basket. He had no idea how true that was.

5

CADE FOCUSED ON the job at hand as best he could with Lexi over there making up his bed. They'd never had sex on it because they could easily have been interrupted. Back then the cabin hadn't been a particularly private spot.

Today, though, it was extremely private. Plus, earlier she'd been ogling his butt. The vacuum made a fair amount of noise, but even so he would have heard the floorboards creak if she'd stepped outside to get the sheets. Those boards were loud, always had been. He and his brothers used to amuse themselves by dancing around the cabin playing those boards like a xylophone.

But he hadn't needed the lack of creaking boards to know she'd been standing there motionless while she watched him clean. He'd been able to sense her gaze on him from the first time they'd met. When he'd leaned over to get the far corner of the mattress, he'd picked up on her little gasp of pleasure, even with the vacuum going.

That little gasp had sent a message straight to his groin. He had a whole slew of mental images that fit that sound, and in all of them she was naked. He'd nearly said to hell with the vacuuming. Now in addition to having a killer headache, his balls ached. If Lexi wanted to, she could help him with both issues, but several things had kept him from asking.

First of all, he was supposed to be thinking about Rosie lying in the hospital. That was his whole reason for being here. Making love to Lexi would make him forget that, which seemed wrong.

Also, he was beyond scruffy. He'd kissed Lexi once with this beard, and he didn't plan to kiss her again until he'd shaved and showered. He was also worried that she'd reject him, and he wasn't mentally in shape for that right now.

Last of all, they had a job to do. Damon and Finn would be here in a few short hours, and he wanted the cabin to be ready.

So instead of trying to seduce her, he'd settled for teasing her. She'd denied ogling him, of course, but they both knew the truth. He could still get her attention. He could build on that, and eventually maybe… No, he wouldn't plan that far ahead and risk jinxing the whole program.

They worked well together, but that was to be expected. They'd shared chores like this for years. When they'd been young teens, their cooperative efforts hadn't been very smooth, but then they'd grown up a little. And he'd kissed her.

From their first kiss on prom night, everything had changed. Suddenly they'd known what to do and how to be with each other. Even though they'd been virgins, sex had been amazing from the beginning. He hadn't appreciated how rare that was until he'd slept with someone else.

He shouldn't be thinking about sex at all with Rosie in the hospital and no word yet about what was wrong with her. But Lexi was right here, her scent swirling in the air as she tucked in sheets and arranged blankets. He'd always felt nothing bad could happen when he was holding her. Good thing they'd never made love in this cabin or he'd be dealing with those memories, too.

She had to stand on a desk chair to make the top bunk, the one Finn would use. Cade kept vacuuming, making sure he got all the nooks and crannies of the windowsills. But he sneaked glances over at her while he worked because she was too beautiful to ignore. She had cut her hair. It was a cap of curls instead of hanging down past her shoulders, but at least she hadn't colored it.

And boy, did she look terrific in jeans. She also looked great out of them. He'd spent many a night admiring the sleek curve of her hips as they tapered to silken thighs. And between those thighs... Ah, he'd spent many happy hours there, too.

He'd loved everything about her—her sharp mind, her bossiness, her laugh, her sentimental streak and her lusty appreciation of sex. He still loved her.

Giving her up had been the toughest choice he'd ever made, but he hadn't been able to provide what she'd wanted. Staying had seemed unfair to both of them. He'd been a little surprised that she hadn't found someone else to fulfill that dream of marriage, a home and kids. He'd braced himself for that eventuality.

Yet here she was, still single. He didn't know what to make of that. Right now his head hurt too damn much to make sense of anything. Thinking about Lexi's hot body probably wasn't helping.

He'd never told another woman that sex could cure his headaches. He didn't know if it would work with anyone besides Lexi because he'd never tested it, as if doing that would be disloyal. Pretty stupid.

He had discovered that solo sex didn't help much at all. Timing his orgasm to match Lexi's, something he'd become fairly good at, had always eliminated his headache completely. Today he'd have to hope that aspirin would do the trick, although he didn't have any. Maybe Lexi could scare up a couple of tablets for him.

"That's it for the beds." She glanced around. "Looking good in here. Want me to vacuum the floor?"

"I can do it."

"I know, but I'll bet you're dying for a shower, and you can take one while I finish up. It'll also give you a chance to see if the washhouse is fit for Damon and Finn."

He grinned. "Don't be so diplomatic. If I stink, just say so."

That made her laugh. "Hit the showers, Gallagher."

"Point taken. So will you still be here when I get back?"

"Sure. I'll wait for you."

"Good. See you in about fifteen minutes." Still smiling, he grabbed a bar of soap, a towel and his duffel before taking the well-worn path to the bathhouse. She was right. A shower and a shave would feel good.

The washhouse could use a good scrub but he'd wait until Finn and Damon were here to help. And because Lexi was waiting for him, he didn't linger. His hair was still damp when he walked back to the cabin carrying his duffel in one hand and his dirty clothes in the other. A close shave and clean clothes had gone a long way toward reviving him. He still had the headache, but he didn't feel grubby anymore.

He'd expected to find Lexi sitting on the front stoop soaking up the sunshine, like the boys used to do when the foster program was still in operation. The laundry basket and the vacuum cleaner were there, though. She'd also shut the door, which was odd. She usually enjoyed this kind of breeze.

When he opened it and stepped inside, he paused in confusion. Lexi's clothes were hanging over the back of a desk chair, and Lexi was…in his bunk. If he wasn't mistaken, and he never was about such things, she was naked under those covers. He lost his grip on the duffel, which fell to the floor with a thud.

She smiled at him. "Let's take care of your headache."

His heart, which had stalled out for a moment, started beating in triple time. It rapidly pumped his blood south, seriously affecting the fit of his jeans. He gulped. "Are you sure about this?"

"Absolutely sure. The only thing I don't know is whether you're packing. If not, then maybe oral—"

"I'm… I have… We're good." She'd short-circuited whatever brain cells had been functioning previously, but animal instincts must have taken over because he found himself ripping off his clothes as if they'd suddenly caught fire. His gaze never left hers as he plopped down on the desk chair and yanked off his boots. "How long have you been planning this?"

"Since we talked in the house."

"Talked about what?" He couldn't imagine how that

conversation had led to *this*. Not that he was complaining. Oh, no. He'd just won the Powerball, and a guy didn't question luck like that.

"You told me sex used to be simple. I didn't see it that way then. But now I do."

"You do?" He wasn't buying it.

"Yes."

"But—"

"Cade, do you want to have a philosophical discussion, or do you want to grab a condom and get into bed with me?"

He grinned. "Let me think about it." He'd said it to make her laugh, which she did, but he wasn't thinking about anything except Lexi's sweet body. He might be making a really big mistake by having sex with her right now. But the spark plugs in his brain weren't firing. And this had been her idea.

So he pulled a condom out of his bag, put it on and walked over to the bunk.

She scooted over to make room for him on the narrow mattress. "Watch your head." Then she drew back the sheet.

He sucked in a breath. Dear God, she was glorious. He'd thought he knew how beautiful she was, but whatever picture he'd carried around for five years, it didn't come close to the reality.

He drank in the sight of her full breasts, her rosy nipples and her narrow waist that flared delicately to hips that shifted under his stare, as if inviting him closer. He let out his breath in a long, reverent sigh. "You're magnificent."

Her voice was soft. "You're not bad yourself."

He glanced into her eyes and discovered she seemed

as absorbed in him as he was in her. What a fool he'd been to leave, and an even bigger fool to stay away. They were made for each other. No one else would do for either of them. That's why she hadn't married someone else. She was a one-man woman, and he was a one-woman man.

She held out her hand. "Come on down here, cowboy. And watch your—"

He whacked his head on the top bunk before she finished the sentence. Lack of sleep and the mesmerizing sight of her lying there waiting for him made him clumsy.

"Oh, Cade."

"It doesn't matter." Nothing mattered but this incredible moment. He climbed in beside her but kept a few inches between them. "Just lie still and let me touch you."

"I want to touch you, too, you know."

He cupped her cheek in one hand and gazed into her eyes. They'd always reminded him of a mountain stream filled with grays and greens and the sparkle of the sun. "I would count it a huge favor if you'd hold off. I'm sizzling like a bottle rocket on the Fourth of July. When I come, I want to be deep inside you."

"Right. Because that's how we'll cure your headache."

"I don't give a damn about my headache." He leaned over and brushed his mouth against hers. "I want to come inside you because it's been so long, and I've missed you so much."

Moaning softly, she clutched the back of his head and pulled him deeper into the kiss.

And he was lost. He'd meant to go slow and reacquaint himself with all the special places he loved, but her tongue was in his mouth, and his was in hers. Before he quite realized it, he'd moved over her and parted her slick thighs.

She was drenched. For him. For *him*. He locked his gaze with hers and murmured her name. Then he plunged deep.

She gasped and rose to meet him, her fingers digging into his back and her eyes flashing fire.

"Lexi." The blood roared in his ears as he thrust into her again and again.

She cried out as the first spasm claimed her. He knew that cry, and once more he drove home, cinching himself in tight, putting pressure where they both needed it. At the exact same moment, they surrendered to the storm. Holding on to each other, they rode it out. Together.

Vaguely he was aware of her soft murmurs as she eased away from him. He didn't want her to leave. He tried to say that, but...he couldn't seem...to stay...awake.

Five minutes later, or so it seemed, her breath was warm against his ear. "Time to wake up, cowboy."

He groaned and stretched his legs. A startled meow and a thump told him he'd just displaced Ringo. Opening his eyes, he looked into Lexi's smiling face.

She perched on the edge of the mattress. "I brought Ringo in a little while ago. I hope you don't mind."

"No, that's great. This is where he needs to be." The gray tabby hopped to the windowsill and peered out the window. "He seems pretty calm."

"He's been no trouble. He let me carry him over here and once I put him down, he jumped up on your bed and settled in."

"Yeah, I used to let him sleep in the bunkhouse in the winter. The guys said I was spoiling him."

"Nothing wrong with that. So, want me to pick up Damon?"

He frowned. "Why?"

"So you can stay here and sleep."

He was still groggy enough to be tempted, but he couldn't let her do that. "I'll get up. Just give me a minute."

"You have at least fifteen." She combed his hair with gentle fingers. "How's your headache?"

"Gone." He rolled onto his back and looked up at her. "I still can't believe you engineered that."

"You needed it. We both did."

Reaching up, he brushed his knuckles over her cheek. "Thank you. That was—"

"Yeah." She held his hand against her cheek as she looked into his eyes. "It was perfect."

"No, not perfect, because that would imply we can't improve on it. As good as that was, we can do even better."

A flush tinged her cheeks. "You think?"

"I know, and so do you. This was a preview, an introduction, an appetizer."

"So you want to do it again sometime?"

"Lexi, be serious."

"Well, I wouldn't mind a repeat, but there are some complications."

Cade sighed as reality intruded. "Yeah, I know."

"Once the three of you are settled in, I might as well head back to my apartment."

"And I'll need to hang with Damon and Finn. Not to mention the main issue of supporting Rosie and Herb in this crisis. That's the whole point of being here. No way am I forgetting that."

"I'll be helping support them, too, so we'll be seeing each other, but we won't have time alone."

He took a deep breath. She was so beautiful. He couldn't believe he'd stayed away so long. "So we're shut down for the time being."

"That's why I decided to go for it now."

He pulled her down until her breath caressed his face. "Thank you," he murmured before capturing her mouth in a kiss that held all the longing in his heart. He could have kept kissing her forever, but she'd mentioned he had fifteen minutes before he had to leave. Reluctantly he let her go. "I'd better get dressed."

"Guess so. You're down to about ten minutes. Do you want me to make you a sandwich to take with you? You must be starving."

He was, but he didn't want her to leave. "That's okay. I'll grab something after I pick up Damon. Would you stay until I have to head out? It might be the last time we can really talk."

"Sure." She settled on one of the desk chairs. Ringo leaped to the desk and offered himself for petting. She obliged. "I don't mind another ogling opportunity."

"So you admit it!" He'd sure love to trade places with that cat.

"It's not every day that a girl sees a virile man wielding a vacuum cleaner. Very arousing."

"I'll have to keep it in mind." He eased out of the bunk bed with more caution than he'd used climbing in. In the process he glanced down and realized that the condom was gone. "Did you…?"

"Yep. You were out like a light, so I took the liberty. It's not like I've never helped you dispose of one before."

"True." He searched the floor for his briefs.

"Looking for these?" She dangled them from one finger.

"Where were they?"

"Caught on the desk lamp." She tossed them to him and went back to stroking Ringo, who was purring loudly.

"On the lamp?"

"You put on quite a show. Clothes flew in all directions. I thought about gathering them up, but I couldn't resist letting you see the chaos you created."

He glanced around. "My God." His shirt hung from the top bunk. His boots had ended up in opposite corners of the room, and his jeans were over by the door. "Where's my hat?"

She pointed to Damon's and Finn's bunks, where his hat had scored a ringer on the bedpost.

"I must have been out of my freaking mind."

Her smile was pure feminine triumph. "As a matter of fact, I think you were."

She was so cute about it that he had to laugh. She'd nailed him, no question, and she had a right to gloat.

But he had something to say, and he didn't want to leave the cabin without saying it. "Okay, so here's the deal." He began pulling on his clothes. "Right now circumstances are preventing us from continuing what we started. Or more accurately, what you started." He paused to look at her.

"I'll own it. I was definitely the instigator."

He nodded, satisfied they were in agreement on that

point. "So you started something, but it isn't finished. Not by a long shot."

She met his gaze. "I hope not."

"Count on it." He'd walked away once. He wasn't planning on repeating that mistake.

6

WHILE CADE FINISHED getting dressed, Lexi remade the bed. Ringo must have taken that as an invitation because he returned to his former spot, curled up and closed his eyes.

Lexi smoothed the wrinkles from the pillowcase. "There. Nobody will be the wiser."

"Except me." Cade pulled on his boots. "I'm a hell of a lot wiser. Two people who make love like that should not be living hundreds of miles apart."

That was the second time he'd hinted at changing his situation. She turned to face him and risked asking the question. "Does that mean you're considering moving back?"

He stood and walked over to retrieve his hat. "It's been on my mind. How would you feel if I did?"

"Herb and Rosie would love it."

Holding his hat by the crown, he settled it on his head, completing the picture of a rugged cowboy. "I assume they would. That isn't what I asked."

She hesitated. Now might be the time to set the record straight. "There's something you should know. I'm not the same person I was five years ago."

"So what? I'm not the same person, either. We'll get reacquainted. Could be fun."

"In my case, my focus has changed. I'm extremely dedicated to my career as a riding instructor."

"I think that's great. You were always good at it."

"That's nice to hear, but it's not the point I'm trying to make." She gazed at him. "Five years ago, I built my schedule, my whole life, really, around you. I'm not willing to do that anymore. Not for you or any guy."

He frowned. "Okay, but we'd see each other, right?"

"Sure. When it's convenient." She was saying it as much for her benefit as his. He was potent, and she couldn't allow his charisma and sex appeal to turn her into the dependent woman she'd been five years ago.

"You're still ticked at me for leaving. I don't blame you, but—"

"I'm not upset about that anymore. In retrospect, it was the best thing that could have happened to me."

He looked as if she'd slapped him. "Is that so? Then maybe I'd better reconsider the idea of moving back. I'd hate to cramp your style."

"I didn't mean it like that. I only meant—"

"If you see me as a potential problem, why the hell did you climb into my bunk this morning?"

"Because I thought it could be simple like you said. No expectations, no agenda, just…"

"Sex." Hurt shone in his green eyes.

"No, it was more than that."

"Damn straight it was. Look, I have to get to the airport, and we both need to concentrate on Rosie, anyway. If and when that settles down, and I have to believe it will or I'll go crazy, we'll compare schedules. Maybe you can fit me in."

"Damn it, Cade! You're being ridiculous."

"Me? You're the one who was wild for me a few hours ago but now you're saying we'll get together when it's *convenient*."

"I was just—"

"Look, I gotta go. Thanks for…everything." He left, closing the door behind him.

Stupid man! She followed him out, making sure the cat stayed inside. Fortunately Ringo seemed uninterested in escape. "I'll probably come to the hospital later," she called out.

"Suit yourself." Cade didn't break stride.

Lexi sighed and leaned against the doorjamb. "That certainly went well." How ironic. Five years ago they'd fought because she'd wanted to marry him and have his babies, but he'd been determined to keep his lone-wolf status.

Now she was the one setting boundaries and he had the hurt feelings. Maybe she shouldn't have used the word *convenient*, but in the end, that was the bottom line. She would no longer drop everything when he beckoned as she'd done during their dating years. He might not have demanded that of her, but it was her pattern. She'd thought they should have an understanding from the get-go that things had changed.

But she'd upset him, and he'd stomped off. Not a good beginning. Maybe she shouldn't have said anything while his nerves were so raw with Rosie in the hospital. He hated hospitals, but he was making himself go there, anyway.

So maybe climbing into his bunk had been a big mistake, except he'd seemed so miserable. Because she'd wanted him, too, she'd thought sex would do them both good. Now she wasn't so pleased about the outcome.

The cabin had an excellent view of the Bighorns from the front stoop, so she stayed where she was and focused on the scenery until she heard Cade's truck drive away. He'd said that their relationship used to be simple. In a flash of insight, she knew why that had been absolutely true. He'd led and she'd followed. Whatever his plan, she'd fallen in with it, at least most of the time.

Who could have blamed her? He was gorgeous, funny and amazing in bed. Making love with Cade was the single most inspiring activity she could imagine. She'd like to do it again, assuming Rosie's health scare turned out to be nothing major and she hadn't ticked him off to the point he'd leave again.

Today's argument aside, she thought the chances of another round of satisfying sex were excellent. Cade wasn't capable of holding a grudge, one of his other endearing qualities. But they hadn't communicated very well regarding this issue. She'd have to try again before they became any more enmeshed.

He was right, though. They wouldn't have much chance to be alone together for the next few days. That would give her time to get her bearings, because she had a feeling he was back to stay.

And she wanted him to. Maybe they'd come to a workable arrangement and maybe they wouldn't, but knowing he'd be around filled her with excitement. Rosie and Herb would be overjoyed.

Imagining how happy they'd be to have one of their boys home again, she started toward the house. She was nearly there when Cade's truck came barreling back in.

He spewed gravel as he braked hard and leaped out, leaving the driver's door open.

"What's wrong?" She hurried to meet him. "Did something happen with Rosie?"

"No, something happened with you and me. We had a damned argument, and it's my fault." He shoved his hat to the back of his head and pulled her into his arms. "I've been home less than twelve hours and I'm already yelling at you, when all I want to do is this." He captured her mouth in a kiss that left no doubt about his feelings.

She wound her arms around his neck and surrendered to the sweet assault of his tongue. Nobody kissed like him. She moaned and invited him deeper.

Shifting his angle, he took all she had to give until they were breathless and frantic. The ridge of his cock pressed hard against her belly as he cupped her backside, his fingers flexing.

Gasping, he lifted his head to gaze down at her. "I want you again, and we can't, and it's driving me crazy."

She managed only one word. "Airport."

"I know." Struggling for breath, he released her and backed away. "I just had to…apologize."

She nodded. "Go." Driving would be painful for a few miles, though.

"Okay." He winced as he climbed into his truck. "That smarts." Closing the door, he started the engine and drove away.

She watched until he was out of sight and she'd stopped quivering. Good Lord, what had she done? Having sex with him this morning had seemed like a good idea at the time, but she should have realized they were playing with dynamite. This time around, though, she would not get burned.

CADE DIDN'T BELIEVE in texting and driving, so he pulled to the side of the road before sending a quick text to Damon to let him know that he was running late but would be there. He added a quick reassurance that Rosie was still doing okay.

He figured that had to be true. Herb would have called or texted if anything major had changed. Cade vowed that from this moment on he'd control his craving for Lexi and concentrate on this deal with Rosie. That remained his top priority.

The craving for Lexi was mostly her fault, so he refused to wallow in guilt over what had happened. Once he'd walked in to find her in his bed—game over. She'd taken away his headache and replaced it with raging lust.

Then she'd come up with that *I'll see you when it's convenient* line. He still figured that was revenge talking, especially after she'd proudly proclaimed that his leaving had been a good thing. Maybe it had. He'd been too young and stupid to make a good husband then.

In his current randy state, he hadn't reacted well to her comments, though. Stomping off had felt great until a mile down the road when he'd realized that he wanted to make love, not war. If he wasn't careful, his ego would take over and he'd lose his chance to be with her.

She had a right to a little revenge. He could take it. But he couldn't take total rejection, not after this morning. He'd thought their vital connection had been broken years ago, but it was still there, maybe even stronger than ever after that long separation.

The mountains had felt welcoming and familiar, but plunging deep into Lexi's warmth had been the ultimate homecoming. He couldn't imagine living here without that mental and physical bond. So he'd driven back to make amends, and he had discovered that just kissing her was no longer an option. Where Lexi was concerned, he wanted it all.

He had a pretty good idea that meant shopping for a ring and setting a date. But that didn't spook him the way it used to. In fact, it sounded kind of nice. He wouldn't broach the subject right away, though.

Once he asked her, she might make him twist in the wind for a while, but that was fair. In any case, she'd wanted a commitment before. Chances were she still did, no matter what she said.

When he reached the airport, he decided not to park. Instead he followed a hunch and cruised past the sidewalk outside the terminal. Sure enough, Damon stood there with a bag slung over his shoulder.

His dark blond hair was a little longer and lighter in color, probably from all that time in the California sun. He wore a trendy pair of shades instead of a Stetson, and a polo instead of a yoked Western shirt, but his jeans were Wranglers and his boots would pass muster in any cowboy bar in the state.

Cade smiled. You could take the man out of the country, but not the country out of the man. A couple of days at Thunder Mountain Ranch and Damon would be back in the saddle looking as if he'd never left.

Pulling up to the curb, Cade beeped the horn.

Damon peered through the windshield, grinned and jogged over to the truck. He climbed in and shoved his bag down by his feet. "Hey, bro."

"Hey, yourself." Cade offered his right hand, and Damon clasped it with the special handshake they'd created for the Brotherhood. "Good to see you."

"Same here. Nice weather you got going on."

"Yeah, it is. Sorry I'm late." Cade checked for traffic and pulled away from the curb.

"No worries. How's Mom?"

"You'll see for yourself pretty soon. I thought we'd go straight there. I'll stay for a bit, and then come back for Finn."

"What time?"

"Three."

"Damn. Too bad we couldn't have coordinated so you wouldn't have to make two trips."

Cade laughed. "Let's think about that. If you'd coordinated, one of you would be riding in back."

"That would have been O'Roarke. My days of getting blown to bits in the back of your truck are over."

"I didn't plan this very well. The three of us have to get home in this truck."

"Then here's an idea. I'll drive, Finn can ride shotgun and you take the back."

"Not likely. My truck. I drive."

"Come to think of it, I'm not sure that's a great idea. By my calculations, you haven't slept much recently."

"I, uh, took a nap this morning." He'd kept thoughts of Lexi at bay for all of three minutes, but now they came rushing back. Damn it, his face felt hot.

Damon peered at him. "You're turning red. What's going on?"

"Nothing."

"Gallagher, you were a lousy liar as a kid, and you haven't improved."

"I don't want to talk about it."

"It's Lexi, isn't it? You said she called you from the ranch house."

"Yeah."

"Okay, I'm piecing this together. You drive to the ranch. Lexi's there. You two have a 'reunion.'" Damon added air quotes to the last part. "How'm I doing so far?"

"You suck."

"Where is she now?"

"She'll probably show up at the hospital later today, but other than that, I don't know." He should have asked her about her plans but he'd been too busy kissing her.

"What do you mean, you don't know? Did you guys have a fight or something?"

"No." Technically they had, but he'd apologized so he imagined the fight had been erased like a drawing on an Etch A Sketch.

"I always liked her."

Cade glared at him. "You did?"

"Not like that, loser. We're the Brotherhood. We don't poach."

"Sorry. My bad."

"Apology accepted, but your reaction tells me all I need to know, including what that so-called *nap* was all about. Pull over and let me drive."

Cade shook his head. "I slept. I swear it."

"*Sleeping* with someone is a figure of speech. Usually very little sleeping goes on. Pull over."

"Sometimes it does."

"Like when?"

"Like this morning. We had sex, and then she left and I slept like a dead person until she woke me up." He glared at Damon. "That stays here, by the way."

"Here, as in the truck? Because eventually Finn will be in this same truck, so technically he should have access to this information."

"Cut me some slack, Harrison. If we spend the next few days discussing Lexi, she'll know it whenever we see her. She's perceptive. And we probably will see her. She wouldn't appreciate being the topic of conversation."

"No, she wouldn't. I wasn't thinking of it from her angle. I won't tell Finn."

"Thank you. Speaking of Finn, have you talked to him recently?"

"It's been a couple of months."

"Same here. I wonder how his microbrewery-slash-tavern is doing."

Damon settled back in the seat. "Last time we talked, he said it was pulling in decent traffic for a start-up, but his divorce didn't help any. Alison demanded a cash settlement, so he's mortgaged to the hilt right now."

"I predict he'll work it out. He knows beer and he likes people. How about you? I see you've gone SoCal with the shades and a knit shirt to show off your manly chest."

Damon laughed. "And I see you're still a shit-kicker wearing the same old beat-up hat."

"You'll wish you had a hat when you're out there raking the corral."

"Can't be much to rake with only a couple of horses."

"Six. Navarre, Isabeau, my horse and three boarders."

Damon stared at him. "Why in hell would they take in boarders? I thought they wanted the easy life."

"Apparently the easy life is boring the hell out of them. That's all I can figure."

"You know, that makes perfect sense. They might have complained a little, but I'll bet they loved being busy. People don't always figure that out when they decide to retire."

Cade braked at a stoplight. "I sure hope the stress of not having enough to do didn't trigger Rosie's problem."

"Who knows? But once she's back home again, we can casually bring up the subject and see what they say."

"Yeah, let's do that. Speaking of being busy, you still like flipping houses?"

"I do, but in this market you can't charge a whole lot or nobody will buy. I don't have what you call liquidity, but I get by okay."

"At least you're not paying out to an unhappy ex."

"No kidding." Damon sighed. "Damn shame about Finn's divorce. When they rushed into it with a Vegas wedding I wondered if it would last."

"Yeah, I know. It seems weird that we never met her and now it's over. Mom seemed to think his wife didn't understand how much time he needed to devote to the business."

"That can be a big problem if you hook up with somebody who expects you home every night at five. It's one of the reasons I haven't let myself get serious about anyone."

Cade laughed. "Don't give me that bullshit. You love playing the field."

"Okay, I do. Besides, unlike you, I never found that perfect matchup."

Cade didn't respond. Although he thought Lexi was perfect for him, he wasn't convinced that he was perfect for her. That *when it's convenient* statement echoed in his head.

"You really do make a great couple. I envy you that. I'll probably end up dancing at your twenty-fifth anniversary party and wondering why I never found the right woman." He glanced over at Cade. "Oh, that's right. You swore you'd never get married. Still feel that way?"

"Not necessarily."

"I knew it! Don't forget to invite me to the wedding."

"We're a hell of a long way from that. I'm not sure she even likes me all that much anymore."

Damon chuckled. "Except when you're horizontal."

"Watch yourself, bro."

"Okay. Touchy subject. I'll back off. Listen, can we stop at a flower shop on the way to the hospital? I'm thinking roses, maybe a few daisies, some—"

"If we brought Mom a vase of flowers, she'd bean us with it. She's convinced that people only bring flowers when they think the patient's a goner."

"Well, hell. You can't walk into a hospital room empty-handed. That's just wrong."

"I can guarantee she doesn't want flowers."

Damon settled back against the seat. "Then we'll have to think of something else."

"Maybe inspiration will hit as we go through town. I need to pick up something to eat. How about you?"

"Yeah, I could use a sandwich. And we should buy some beer to take back to the house. I don't intend to drink up Dad's supply while I'm here."

Cade glanced at him. "I know what we can get Mom."

"Beer? I don't think she likes—"

"Not beer. Something better."

And that was how Cade and Damon ended up walking into Rosie's room carrying a case of Baileys Irish Cream.

"My God!" Rosie's eyes widened. "It'll take years for me to drink all that booze!"

"And that," said Damon as he leaned down to kiss her cheek, "is the whole point."

7

LEXI STAYED AT the ranch until dinnertime so she could feed the horses and the cat before going to the hospital. Herb had called to ask if she'd bring the paperback romance Rosie had been reading. She'd never been much for TV.

Herb had sounded tired but joyful because his boys were home. He'd mentioned that friends had been dropping by the hospital, and he seemed gratified by that, too. Rosie knew a ton of people, and word of what she called her *incarceration* had spread.

Her test results wouldn't be available for at least another day, so the hospital staff had rolled a cot into her room for Herb. He'd shyly asked if Lexi would pack a few essentials for him in an overnight bag.

Such a devoted husband, she thought while tucking clean underwear and a fresh shirt in the small suitcase. Fortunately his toiletries were all located on one side of the double sink in the master bath and Rosie's were on the other. Lexi easily figured out which toothbrush was his. She added toothpaste, shaving cream, his razor and some men's deodorant.

At the last minute she remembered pajamas. He hadn't asked for them, but he'd be happier trying to sleep at the hospital if he had some. She opened several drawers before she found a pair with the price tags still attached. She took off the tags and packed the PJs. From all the evidence, he wasn't in the habit of wearing any.

Herb had never had daughters, or he'd probably own several pairs. She was the closest thing he had to a daughter, but still, she could imagine his reluctance to ask her for this favor. She was glad he'd summoned the courage. A crisis was always easier to deal with in clean clothes.

After hauling his little case and her own out to her truck, she went back inside for one last pass through the house. She wiped down the kitchen counters and refolded the afghan over the back of the couch. Then she fluffed the throw pillows and turned on a couple of lamps to welcome the guys when they arrived.

They'd sleep in the cabin for old times' sake, but first they'd probably sit around the kitchen table, drinking beer and catching up. They might even play some pool or get out a deck of cards. She wished she could be here. She'd love to find out what Damon and Finn were doing these days.

But she wasn't a member of the Thunder Mountain Brotherhood. And she had this explosive situation with Cade. She couldn't complain about that because she'd created it with her bright idea this morning.

Seeing him at the hospital shouldn't be a problem, but her pulse rate climbed as she drove there. She focused her thoughts on Rosie. Somehow she'd transform Cade's presence into background noise. If she didn't accomplish that, Rosie would be the first to notice. Rosie had been hoping for their reconciliation ever since the breakup.

She was the other person Lexi needed to talk with, but that would have to wait until the health crisis had passed. Rosie had expected a wedding five years ago, too. She'd dropped casual comments about having it at the ranch, maybe even on horseback.

If Cade mentioned moving back, and he might already have said something, Rosie might start hearing wedding bells again. At some point Lexi needed to tell her that marriage to Cade—or anyone, for that matter—was no longer her dream. Rosie was a progressive thinker, so she'd accept that.

The hospital parking lot was crowded, but Lexi's gaze was drawn to Cade's black truck. He'd had that truck for ten years, which meant she'd made love to him in the back of it. To avoid being reminded of those steamy episodes, she parked as far away as possible.

She had no trouble finding Rosie's room because of the small crowd gathered outside. Cade stood in one conversational group that included Herb, Damon and Finn. On the other side of the door were Lexi's mom and two women who'd worked in social services with Rosie.

Rosie's door was open, but the curtain had been pulled around her bed. Lexi decided the reason for that must be a routine procedure or the people standing outside wouldn't be talking and joking with each other. She waved at her mom before wheeling the suitcase over to Herb. The poor guy needed what she'd brought him. Normally well-groomed, he looked the worse for wear.

He gave her a hug. "You're an angel. I'm getting to the point where I can't stand myself, so I can't imagine how everybody else is putting up with me."

"We're rough, tough cowboys," Cade said. "We can go days without a bath or a shave."

Lexi managed not to laugh. Cade had been desperate for a shower only hours ago.

"Speak for yourself, Gallagher." Damon came over to hug Lexi. "How're you doing, beautiful?"

"I'm doing well." She hugged him back. "Apparently California agrees with you. You're all tan and stuff."

"And *stuff*?" Cade laughed. "What's that supposed to mean?"

"That you're transforming into Thor." Finn came over for his hug. "You might think that 'flipping houses' is about fixing them up for resale, but I think he literally tosses them around."

"Says the guy who's turned into a vampire." Damon gestured toward Finn. "Look at how pale this guy is and tell me I'm wrong."

Lexi surveyed Finn. He was a little paler than he'd been while living on the ranch, but his brilliant blue eyes and dark hair had been attracting female attention ever since he'd hit puberty. "Vampires are considered sexy these days."

Finn smiled. "I could always count on you, Lex."

She'd forgotten that. In the early days of the Thunder Mountain Brotherhood, Finn hadn't been quite sure of himself. Cade and Damon had been impatient with his tentative nature, but she'd been his champion. She'd listened to his stories about his beloved grandfather, the man who'd taken him in and who'd longed to own his own tavern. But Grandpa O'Roarke had no business sense and a bad heart. Finn honored his memory with his Seattle microbrewery and tavern. She found that incredibly sweet.

Two nurses filed out of the room. "You can go back in," said the taller one, "but you might want to take turns. All of you at once could be a bit overwhelming."

"I vote for Lexi to go in by herself," Herb said. "She's the only one who hasn't seen Rosie yet, and Rosie's been asking for her."

"Good idea," Cade said immediately.

Lexi appreciated both the opportunity and Cade's support. He knew more than anyone that Rosie was like a second mother to her. He'd heard the panic in her voice when she'd called him after Herb had taken Rosie to the hospital. Ever since then, Lexi had worked hard to maintain a positive attitude, but worry had taken its toll. Seeing Rosie alone would go a long way to calming her fears.

When she walked in, Rosie's face lit up. "Lexi! Oh, thank God."

"What's the matter?" Alarmed, she hurried over to Rosie's bedside and pulled up a chair.

Rosie lowered her voice. "I don't know where to start. Pull that chair closer."

"Are you feeling worse?" Lexi scooted right up next to the bed. "Should I call someone?"

"Absolutely not. Herb knew I wanted to talk to you alone, so he asked you to bring that book."

"I have it right here." She pulled it out of her purse.

"That's fine. Thanks." She took it and laid it aside. "I'll read it tonight after everybody leaves, but I wanted to make sure you came."

"Of course I would! I've been dying to see you!" Then she heard what she'd said. "I mean *eager* to see you."

Rosie waved a dismissive hand. "You don't have to

watch what you say. I'm not dying, but Herb and I are in a financial mess. And now the boys are here, and I'm afraid they'll go off the deep end. I'm counting on you to keep them from doing anything stupid."

"Wait, does this have anything to do with those horses you're boarding?" Lexi's stomach churned. It seemed a bad situation was about to get worse.

"That was a stopgap measure, back when we thought every little bit would help. Ten months ago one of our dear friends, Hector Williams, was in a terrible financial bind, but it was supposed to be temporary."

"I know Hector. I taught his daughter how to ride. Nice guy."

"He's a very nice guy." Rosie took a deep breath. "He only needed a boost for a short time. Three months. We didn't want to pull money from our retirement account, so we took out a second mortgage on the ranch with a balloon payment due this September. It should have been fine."

"Let me guess. He can't repay you, after all."

"No, he can't. He was laid off and can't find work. But we weren't too worried. We had the retirement money we could use if necessary."

Lexi felt the chill of impending doom.

"We tried to withdraw funds from our account and kept getting the runaround. Then last week we finally got an answer regarding our investment. It was a Ponzi scheme, Lexi. The money's gone."

"No."

"We couldn't believe it, either. The government's prosecuting and eventually we may get some of it back, but there's no telling if or when."

"But how could that happen? You two have always

been so careful!" She realized she was talking too loudly and toned it down. "I can't believe you put all your savings in a Ponzi scheme. That's not you."

"We trusted our financial planner, who is also a really great person, but he was fooled. He feels terrible, but there's not much he can do. He has several clients in the same boat. We're wiped out. And if we can't come up with the balloon payment in September, we'll lose the ranch."

Lexi was unable to speak as images of the beloved place with its treasured memories flashed through her mind.

"You're in shock, and that's not surprising. So were we."

Lexi wondered if this had caused Rosie's episode, whatever it turned out to me. But she saw no reason to point that out. Rosie had probably thought of it herself. Instead she focused on being positive. "There's a solution to this. We just have to find it."

"Maybe there is a solution, although I don't know what it is. I'm telling you because eventually the boys will find out, and I'm afraid they'll go overboard in their attempt to save the ranch. I picture Finn selling his business and Damon liquidating all his current projects whether they're finished or not. Cade doesn't have a lot to sell, so I'm not sure what he'd do. Become a gigolo, maybe."

That surprised a giggle out of Lexi.

Rosie smiled. "He'd be great at it."

"No doubt. And for you and Herb, he might consider it."

"He might at that, but we can't let any of that happen. Damon and Finn need to continue on the path they've chosen, and I keep hoping you and Cade… Well, that's a discussion for another time. Maybe we should sell the ranch and cut our losses."

"Is that what you want?" Lexi held her breath. She couldn't blame them if they made that decision. Thunder Mountain Ranch was a big responsibility even with money available to run it. Struggling to hold things together in the face of financial disaster wasn't something a couple in their sixties needed.

"I'm not sure." Rosie smoothed the covers. "Neither is Herb. But we can't have those boys sacrificing a promising future to prop us up. If I hadn't landed in the hospital, they never would have found out about any of it, but I had this little incident. The truth is going to come out."

"And it should. Right now Cade thinks you just want to stay busy, but if you're really in danger of losing the ranch…they deserve to know."

"You're right." Rosie's features softened. "How are things going between you two? I can't tell from Cade's behavior."

For the first time since she'd pulled up a chair next to Rosie's bed, Lexi glanced away.

"Complicated, huh?"

"Yes." She met Rosie's warm gaze. "But not so complicated that I can't help you with this. Much as I love Thunder Mountain Ranch, I agree that they shouldn't sacrifice everything for it. And that might be their first impulse."

"I know, and you could talk them out of it. They all respect you."

"Rosie, they respect *you*. If you tell them not to be foolish, then—"

"They'll ignore me and do it anyway, for my sake. Did you see the case of Baileys in the corner?"

Lexi hadn't noticed, but when she glanced over, sure enough, there it sat. "They bought you a case of Baileys?"

"Cade and Damon arrived with it this afternoon in lieu of flowers. I shouldn't have ranted about not wanting flowers, because a bouquet would have been a heck of a lot cheaper than all that booze. Anyway, you see how they are."

"Yeah." Lexi smiled as she pictured Cade and Damon coming up with that idea and then proudly bringing the box into the hospital room.

"I figure you might have a better shot at convincing them that throwing away all they've worked for would not make me happy and grateful. It would make me mad as a hornet."

Lexi nodded. "I can see how it would."

"You understand because you're a woman and you think like a woman. Those three, bless their hearts, think like men, and men are prone to fall on their swords for the glory of the cause. Even Herb has a touch of that. If he could come up with a grand gesture at great personal cost, he'd do it without another thought."

Lexi smiled. "You're right. He would."

"Don't get me wrong. I love those guys with all my heart, but I don't trust their judgment when it comes to something like the ranch. It sheltered the Brotherhood from the storm. I know it did, and they have a right to be sentimental about it, but not if it means giving up everything they've worked for."

"Exactly." Lexi studied Rosie. "So how are you feeling? Because you look pretty perky to me."

"To be honest, seeing those three boys has done me a world of good. Also, I wasn't eating right. And worrying interferes with your digestion, too. I've been feeling stronger every minute. I'm viewing this as a warning not to let this situation take me—or anyone I love—down."

"Understood. But what's next? Are you planning to tell them or just let them find out by themselves? They will, you know. They won't leave town without figuring it out."

"And Cade's not leaving at all."

Lexi blinked. "He told you that?"

"Didn't have to. He could stay away as long as he didn't come back for a visit. But now that he's home, the glue is taking hold. The other two boys, I'm not so sure. But then again, they didn't leave a sweetheart here."

"Rosie, don't get your hopes up about—"

"I won't, I won't. I have enough to keep me busy without obsessing about you and Cade. As to your question, I'd like you to tell them. Tonight."

"Tonight?" Her voice squeaked in surprise.

"I know it's a big thing to ask, but I'd like you to drive back with them and have a powwow around the kitchen table. You know they'll have a powwow with or without you. I want you to be a part of it. And break the news."

"Oh, Rosie, I don't know. I think they'd rather hear it from you or Herb."

"Not necessarily. If one of us tells them, they'll have to be careful what they say. If you tell them, they'll be free to cuss and carry on as much as they want. I've been thinking about this ever since Cade showed up this morning, and you're the right messenger. I'm sure of it."

"That makes some sort of crazy sense." Lexi had wanted to be part of the reunion tonight, anyway, but now she'd come bearing bad news. She might not be a welcome guest for long.

"Besides, they have a slight transportation problem. I've heard them arguing about it. If all three of them ride home in Cade's truck, one of them has to go in the back or they have to somehow cram into the front. Damon and Finn aren't happy about either option. If you go, too, you can remedy that situation."

"What if they don't want me there?"

"I personally think they'd love to have you there, but if you're worried about it, just offer to give Damon or Finn a ride to the ranch. They'll invite you to stay for a drink and you're golden."

"Okay. I'll do it. Now I'd better make way for the horde outside your door. It's getting to be standing room only out there. I'm waiting for the fire department to show up and start ushering people out of the hallway."

Rosie laughed, and suddenly she looked about twenty-five. "I'm not the least bit happy about ending up here, and the hospital gowns couldn't be less flattering, but I love getting to see all my friends. And having my guys show up is fantastic, as long as they don't screw up their lives as a result."

"I'll do what I can." Lexi pushed back her chair. "I'm a little intimidated but honored that you'd trust me with this."

"I've known you since you were a little kid. I'd trust you with my life."

Unexpected tears sprang to Lexi's eyes. She gave Rosie a quick hug and hoped she hadn't noticed the waterworks. "Same here."

"Rosie, I hate to interrupt." Herb walked into the room. "But we have a situation out there and I thought you'd want to know about it."

Rosie pushed a button that propped her upright, as if she'd be able to face the news better that way. "What sort of situation?"

"As you know, the word's out that you're in the hospital."

"I'm aware of that."

"So Ben dropped by."

"Ben's here?" Lexi would definitely say hello. The saddle he'd made her last year was the best one she'd ever owned.

Herb nodded. "And he brought Molly."

Rosie gasped and clapped a hand to her mouth.

"What's wrong with that?" Lexi stared at her in confusion. Ben and Molly had married this past spring at the Last Chance Ranch in Jackson Hole. Molly was the Chance brothers' cousin, and thanks to her, Lexi was conducting a riding clinic over there in mid-July.

Rosie ignored the question as she looked at Herb. "Has she met Cade?"

"Yep."

"Has she figured it out?"

"Yep."

"I need to go out there." Rosie started to get out of bed.

"No, you don't." Herb hurried over to stop her. "The horse is out of the barn. We'll let them work through it. I just thought I'd better tell you."

"I should've called that boy the minute I met Molly. It's obvious the two of them are related. But things have been so crazy."

"Related?" But immediately Lexi knew it was true. That explained why she'd liked Molly on sight. She'd looked into Molly's green eyes and had felt as if they already knew each other.

Rosie glanced over at her. "Molly's maiden name is Gallagher."

"It is?" Lexi hadn't met her until after she'd married Ben, so she'd had no reason to know that.

"I've kept quiet about this because it was so sensitive, but she called before Christmas looking for lost relatives. She asked if I knew anything about a family named Marlowe. I could honestly say I didn't."

"I guess that's true." Cade had mentioned that after Rance Marlowe had abandoned them, they'd started using his mom's maiden name, which had suited them both just fine.

"Anyway, I took Molly's number and passed it on to Cade."

"And he didn't call."

"Guess not."

Lexi wasn't surprised. She'd once asked him if he'd tried to contact his mother's family. Apparently he'd decided at a young age that if his mom had avoided them, they must be as worthless as his dad was.

Rosie sighed. "Long story short, I'm guessing Molly and Cade are first cousins."

"Which means Cade is also a first cousin of the Chance brothers." Lexi had trouble digesting that. She couldn't imagine what Cade must be feeling right now. The Chance family was well-known in Wyoming for their registered Paints, their beautiful ranch and their community spirit.

Cade's self-image had always been that of a lone

wolf. Although he was extremely loyal to his foster parents and his two adopted brothers, he'd also taken a perverse pride in being a guy with no typical family ties. That was about to change.

8

CADE LOOKED INTO eyes the same shade of green as his. She wore tortoiseshell glasses, but behind those glasses were eyes that were achingly familiar. His mother's eyes. Molly's earnest explanation wasn't registering, but the sound of her voice mesmerized him. She sounded just like his mother, too.

Somewhere in his duffel he had Molly Gallagher's phone number, but he'd never bothered to call. Apparently she was Molly Gallagher Radcliffe now, because she was married to Ben, the saddle maker Rosie adored. He couldn't make sense of how everything fit together. But as the fog slowly cleared from his brain, Molly's words began to penetrate.

"I should have guessed that you'd ditch your father's name and take your mother's maiden name, but somehow that never occurred to me. So you *were* at Thunder Mountain Ranch."

"Yes." His lips felt numb.

"So that means your mother—"

"Died when I was thirteen. In this hospital. Cancer."

She looked stricken. "I'm so sorry. But you're here! We thought we'd lost you forever!"

He swallowed. "We?"

"All of us! My mom, my dad, my aunts and uncles, my brothers, my cousins, my nieces and nephews. You have so much family in Arizona that you won't believe it. And in Wyoming! Have you heard of the Last Chance Ranch over in Jackson Hole?"

He shrugged, trying valiantly to stay cool while his emotions rode a stomach-dropping roller coaster. "Sure. Who hasn't?"

"The Chance brothers are my cousins, and that means they're also your cousins! Is that wild or what?"

Cade struggled to take it all in. To think the Gallaghers had been upset that he and his mother had lost touch with them. They'd tried to pick up the trail, but they'd been looking for Heather and Cade Marlowe. The Gallaghers didn't sound like losers at all, and Molly seemed nice.

He'd never questioned why his mother had cut off contact, but now he had a pretty good idea what had made her do it. She'd been ashamed of how her life had turned out, and she hadn't wanted her parents or her siblings to know how bad things were. From the sound of it, the Gallaghers were a prosperous and upstanding family. And the Chances—most everybody in this area knew about them.

Rance Marlowe had beaten and belittled Cade's mother until she'd lost all confidence in herself. She'd probably thought she wasn't good enough to be in the company of such people as the Gallaghers and the Chances. She'd died without telling him much of anything about his heritage, and if Molly hadn't come along, he still wouldn't know.

Molly put a hand on his arm. "It's a lot to absorb all at once."

"Yeah." He took a shaky breath. "So your family lives in Prescott? Is that what you said?"

"Yes, they're ranchers." She hesitated. "I'd love to tell them I found you, but you might not be ready for that."

Her husband, who'd been standing quietly beside her through the whole drama, slipped an arm around her waist. "You should probably give him a little time to adjust."

"I'll second that." Herb appeared and stood beside Cade. "Must be tough, going from no relatives at all to a whole passel of them."

About that time Cade realized that not a single person standing in the hallway was talking. This little drama had been a real conversation stopper. Lexi stood in Rosie's doorway, and she looked worried. He glanced around at the others and saw concern and sympathy on every face, including Janine's. He must look truly bushwhacked if Lexi's mother felt sorry for him.

Enough of that nonsense. Nobody had to feel sorry for Cade Gallagher. He could handle whatever came at him. Reaching deep, he pulled out a smile. "You know, it would be tough if I'd just found out that I'm related to a bunch of criminals, but come on. Judging from Molly, the Gallaghers must be really cool, and the Chances are like royalty around here. The way I look at it, I'm a damned lucky guy."

Molly brightened. "So I can let my parents know you're here and I've talked to you?"

"Absolutely." His stomach hurt like hell. They'd want

to know about his mom and maybe even his worthless dad. He'd have to relive things he was trying to forget.

"They'll invite you down to Arizona."

"And I'd be honored to go." Someday. Far in the distant future. He tried not to think about it.

"The Chances will probably invite you over there, too."

"That'd be great." The pain in his stomach rolled. He hoped he wouldn't embarrass himself by throwing up. "So, now that's all settled, we should probably draw straws for who gets to go see Rosie next."

"You go," Herb said. "I'm sure she wants to apologize."

"For what?"

"Not contacting you about Molly!" Rosie called from her bed.

That got him moving. He hurried into the room. "You knew about this?"

"Not for absolute sure, but when I met her, I couldn't stop looking at her eyes. Of course, I couldn't say anything to her about you without your permission. I kept meaning to call you, but…I got distracted. I'm sorry, Cade. That was a rough way to find out."

He walked over to the bed and squeezed her hand. "It's okay." Then he thought about what she'd said. "So what distracted you?" Must have been significant if she hadn't called him about Molly.

"Oh, various things. Listen, I'm getting tired and I know Herb must be pooped. How about sending people in one at a time so I can tell them good-night and then all of you can take off. It's been a long day."

"I know. You've probably had way too much excitement and way too much company."

"Doesn't seem to have hurt me. My excellent nurses said my vitals were good this last time. I predict I'll be home tomorrow."

"That would be terrific."

"It would." She smiled at him. "Now line 'em up and move 'em out, cowboy."

When he made the announcement, everyone cooperated beautifully. He leaned against the wall and waited for Damon and Finn, who wanted to be last. He was tired, but not as much as he probably should be. All the excitement Molly had stirred up still fizzed in his brain.

Lexi walked over. "I need to talk to you a minute."

"Sure." He hadn't had any time with her since she'd arrived, which was probably a good thing because even now, with so many people around, he had a strong urge to hold her. That would go a long way toward steadying him.

"How're you doing with this Molly thing?"

"Okay, I guess." Then he had an unpleasant thought. "Please tell me you didn't know about it. Because if you knew and didn't tell me, I—"

"I didn't know. I swear I would have warned you."

He sighed in relief. "Good."

"Are you really okay about it?"

"I should be overjoyed, don't you think?"

She studied him with those hazel eyes that saw so much. "I don't know. It definitely changes things if you suddenly have a bunch of relatives you didn't know about. That could take some getting used to."

"Yeah." He let out a long breath. "To tell the truth, it knocked me for a loop. The idea of meeting all those people… Well, I'll deal with that later. But for sure one thing won't change. Thunder Mountain Ranch will always be home."

Her gaze flickered. "Right."

"Okay, what's going on?"

"I need to talk to all three of you. I've found out a few things."

He didn't like the way she said that, as if it wouldn't be news he'd want to hear, but news that he'd have to hear. "Can you just tell me now?"

"I'd rather explain it to all three of you at once and in a more private setting than this."

"You're starting to worry me, Lex."

"Look, just go with it. Besides, if I drive my truck back to the ranch, then either Damon or Finn can ride with me so you don't have to fight about who ends up in the back of yours."

"Rosie told you about that, did she?"

"You know Rosie. She hears all."

Cade laughed. "She always did. Can't get away with a damned thing around her. Okay. Sounds as if we need to hear whatever you dug up. I hated the idea that I wouldn't see you tonight, anyway." Somehow his hand had come in contact with hers, and he began gently stroking the back of it with one finger. Touching her, even that little bit, calmed him. But the longer he did it, the more he wanted to pull her into his arms and kiss that beautiful mouth.

His touch must have affected her, too, because her eyes darkened and she took a ragged breath. "I'll drive out there because it's the best place for us to relax and talk, but you and I won't be doing anything."

"I know." Not unless they got creative. He was already mentally working on the problem.

"I mean it, Cade. You have that gleam in your eye."

"No, I don't." He blinked and tried to look innocent. "See? No gleam."

"You need to hang out with Damon and Finn. I'll probably only stay for an hour or so."

"Okay." He held off dreaming up potential make-out spots because she could read his mind. But he wasn't about to have her drive all the way out there without at least the possibility of a few kisses. And maybe a little fondling. And maybe—

"The gleam's back, Gallagher." She sounded as if she wanted to laugh but was trying to be stern. "Cut it out."

"Have pity on me. This morning some hot woman got me all stirred up, and I can't seem to put her out of my mind."

She rolled her eyes. "If I'd known how that would affect you, I would have—"

"Done it anyway, I hope. That was epic. One for the record books."

"Yes, but now you're all wound up with no outlet."

"Don't worry. I'll figure it out." And now that Rosie seemed to be improving, he didn't feel quite so guilty for thinking about getting horizontal with Lexi. Rosie was still his main focus, although Rosie would be delighted to know that he and Lexi still got along.

He glanced toward Rosie's door as Finn came out. He reluctantly stopped stroking Lexi's hand and pushed away from the wall. "Hey, O'Roarke, this lovely lady has offered to drive you to the ranch so you won't have to arm wrestle Harrison for the passenger seat of my truck."

"Sounds good to me." Finn smiled at her. "I hope you're coming in for a beer, although I have to warn you, it's not up to my standards. At least it'll be cold. We picked up a Styrofoam cooler and loaded it with ice."

"I'd love to share a beer with you guys."

Cade studied Finn and shook his head. "I don't know about this vampire thing, but you've turned into a beer snob, for sure. There's nothing wrong with the beer we got."

"Come to Seattle and have a glass of O'Roarke's Pale Ale and you'll be converted on the spot. Once you've tasted my brew, you won't be satisfied with anything else."

"That would be damned inconvenient, now wouldn't it? I can't be driving to Seattle every time I want a beer."

"I'm working on that. Eventually I'll have wider distribution. Give me another year or two, and you'll be seeing my label all over the place."

"If you're spreading something all over the place," Damon said as he came out of Rosie's room, "I'm gonna watch where I step."

Finn scowled. "Nice talk in front of a lady, Harrison."

"Lex can take it." Damon grinned at her. "I'd say you're just like one of the guys, but you're a lot prettier than any of us. Right, Gallagher?"

"Right." Cade trusted Damon, but he couldn't seem to help flirting with every woman he met. That was why Cade wanted Finn in Lexi's truck and Damon in his. He was feeling a little vulnerable, and he didn't want to imagine Damon charming Lexi all the way back to the ranch. "In fact, Lexi's coming back with us so she can fill us in on a few things. Finn's riding with her and you're with me."

"Perfect. Now there won't be any bloodshed over who sits where. Thanks, Lex."

"My pleasure. How about we pick up pizza on the way back? We can call it in once we get going, and it should be ready by the time we get there."

Cade loved it when she took charge like that. He'd loved it this morning, too. "Is that place we like still open?"

"It is. So one family size with everything on it?"

Damon closed his eyes. "Oh, yeah. I can taste it already. Let's go."

Cade led the way, checking the rearview mirror constantly. When they stopped for the pizza, Finn and Lexi took it in their truck and promised not to snitch any. Lexi seemed to be having a great time talking to Finn, which was fine. Cade had never been the jealous type, but that was before, when nobody had touched Lexi the way he had.

She'd had other lovers since then, and now he saw rivals around every corner. Not his brothers, obviously, who would never make a move on his girl. But what if Lexi took a liking to either Finn or Damon? He hadn't been able to imagine that when they were dating. Now he could.

Damon glanced at him. "You're not really worried that they'll eat the pizza, are you?"

"Nah."

"Just wondering. If I had a dollar for every time you've checked your mirror I'd have enough to cover the pizza and a tank of gas."

"You're right. I'm being ridiculous." He forced himself to stop glancing in the mirror.

"You're going to have to marry that woman."

"I know."

"Will she have you?"

"Maybe. Maybe not. She's still pissed about me leaving five years ago. She announced that she'd see me when it was convenient."

"Ouch."

"It's okay. I don't blame her for wanting me to suffer a little."

"Then suffer for her. Hell, you're already suffering. Want me to tell her that?"

"Please don't."

"Okay. So what about this deal with you being related to everybody in the known universe? You looked a little freaked by the news."

"Wouldn't you be?"

"You bet I would. Since I ran away from home to escape my parents, if they or anyone related to them showed up, I'd shit a brick. But this isn't Rance Marlowe we're talking about. This is the good side of the family. I didn't have a good side. Everybody was rotten."

"I've fantasized about tracking him down and beating him to a bloody pulp. He essentially killed my mother, even though he was long gone when she died." Being at the hospital where she'd died, along with the news from Molly, had brought those thoughts back. Cade tried not to think about his father at all, but right now he couldn't help it.

"I don't blame you, but you'd be a young guy beating up on an old guy, and it would be your word against his that he deserved it. You could end up in jail and for what? You can't bring your mother back."

"Justice."

"From what you've told me, I'm thinking he has a

miserable life if he's even still around. A hard drinker who likes picking fights could be dead by now."

"I hope he is, the bastard. He made her feel like she wasn't good enough for her own family."

Damon was quiet for a while. Finally he broke the silence. "Are you afraid that you're not good enough?"

The question arrowed into his gut. Damon always had been able to cut to the chase. "Yeah," he said at last. "I am."

9

ONLY CADE SUSPECTED that Lexi had bad news to report, and he seemed in no rush to delve into it yet. So she decided to let the matter rest for a while as they lounged around the kitchen table and enjoyed their reunion.

Damon and Finn had insisted that Cade had to fetch his cat, so Ringo lay purring happily in Cade's lap while the conversation grew louder and more animated. The four of them had shared some hilarious moments, and those memories were even funnier now.

Lexi had been acutely conscious of Cade's absence over the years, but until now she hadn't realized how much she'd missed watching him interact with Damon and Finn. They were great guys, and she admired all three of them for rising above less-than-ideal beginnings. Rosie and Herb had certainly helped them bounce back, but they'd had to do a lot of the character work on their own.

Not having Rosie and Herb at the table seemed strange, but after a comment or two about that, nobody brought it up again. Wishing they were there wouldn't make it so. Instead the guys talked about pranks they'd pulled on the younger boys that had come and gone—the ones they'd liked and the ones who had been a pain in the ass.

"We should get them all back here," Damon said. "Even the PITAs. I know Rosie has contact information for every kid she took in. Wouldn't that be a kick?"

"Maybe not for Rosie and Herb," Lexi said. "It would be a lot of work. And we can't expect them to do it, especially now."

"So we'd hire people to help out." Damon finished his beer and got up to take another out of the fridge. "Anyone else?"

"Hit me." Finn grabbed a slice of the quickly disappearing pizza. "Are you saying you have money to throw into the pot, Harrison? Because I don't. My card is maxed out after paying for my plane ticket."

"We could do the work," Cade said. "I can handle a vacuum." He winked at Lexi.

She ducked her head to hide her expression. *The rat.* She'd been focusing on the camaraderie, mostly. She'd chosen a seat across the table from him in hopes the distance would lessen his impact.

But that had given her a better view, and he was too damned good-looking to ignore. Plus his warm chuckle made her shiver, and, as he stroked the cat, she imagined him stroking her. When he laughed she remembered the moment she'd fallen for him at sixteen. As if she'd been struck by lightning, she'd never been the same. And she'd always love Cade.

"I can clean." Damon glanced at Lexi. "Why're you studying the grain of the table, girl? Are you afraid we'll expect you to cook and clean because you're the female of the group?"

She glanced up and cleared her throat. "Nope. Herb and Rosie taught you guys well. You don't think like that." A sip of beer and she was back in control of herself.

"Damn straight. You wouldn't have to do diddly-squat unless you want to." Damon snapped his fingers. "I've got it! You can be our Reunion Queen. How's that? We'll get you a tiara."

"Actually, I have one."

"You do?" Cade smiled. "I did not know that."

"You don't know everything about me." *Whoops.* Probably shouldn't have said *that*. "I got it after you left," she added quickly.

"Did somebody give it to you?" His question sounded casual, but obviously he wanted to know if a guy had.

"As a matter of fact, I bought it for myself. My friends and I decided we needed tiaras. We wear them sometimes when we meet for drinks."

"Interesting idea." Cade seemed a little lost.

She'd bet it sounded odd to him that she'd put on a tiara and have drinks with her girlfriends. She wouldn't have dreamed of doing such a thing five years ago. But that was the point. She'd changed.

"Well, there you go." Finn glanced from Cade to Lexi as if trying to figure out the subtext of their conversation.

She'd avoided discussing Cade during the drive to the ranch. Instead she'd encouraged Finn to talk about his business.

Damon set down his beer bottle. "So! Our Reunion Queen has a tiara and the three of us will cook and clean for the event. We have a plan, but we have to move on it immediately. I don't know about you, O'Roarke, but I can only stay a week."

"Same here. But we can get the info from Rosie tomorrow. It might turn out that some of the guys live within driving distance."

Lexi decided the time had come to face reality. "Before this idea gets any more solid, you all need to know something."

Finn panicked. "Shit! Rosie's dying."

"No, she's not! Settle down." She hadn't thought about how scary heart attacks might be for Finn. "I'll bet this'll turn out to be a warning for her more than anything. *But* Rosie and Herb are in serious financial trouble. Enough so that they could lose the ranch."

Shock registered on all three faces. Then Damon and Finn started cussing, just as Rosie had predicted they might.

But Cade sighed. "I was afraid of that when you said you had important news." He looked across the table at her. "And you'd just had that heart-to-heart with Rosie."

"I don't get it." Damon sounded frustrated. "They were fine last time I asked, not that long ago. I don't see how it could end up this way in such a short time."

"That's what I'm here to explain." Lexi proceeded to repeat what Rosie had told her about the loan to Hector Williams followed by the discovery of the Ponzi scheme. The expressions around the table grew darker by the minute.

When she was finished, Cade was the first to lash out. "Who is the scumbag who cheated all those people? I want his name, damn it! And where he lives!" Startled, Ringo leaped down.

"Now you've done it," Damon said. "You scared the

cat." He patted his thigh. "Come on over here, Ringo. I won't yell like that other guy."

Tail in the air, Ringo bypassed Damon and joined Lexi.

Finn nodded approvingly. "Smart cat." Then he glanced at Cade. "I understand where you're coming from, bro, but knowing that information won't help. That type protects themselves with crooked lawyers and soulless accountants. He probably lives on some private island in the Caribbean."

Cade blew out a breath. "Yeah, I'm sure you're right."

"I watched this play out with one of my grandfather's supposed investments." Finn got up and went to the refrigerator. "Anybody need another beer?"

"Sure do." Cade pushed aside his empty bottle.

Finn returned with two beers and handed one to Cade. "Eventually the bad guys go to jail, and maybe the people they swindled will get some of the money back, but not soon enough to do them any good. What I want to know is whether Hector Williams has assets he can sell."

Lexi had wondered about that, too. "I didn't ask because it sounded as if she had no interest in trying to get the money from him. He's out of work and he has a family."

Finn sat down again. "And I feel sorry for him, but if he has assets, he needs to liquidate them ASAP and pony up the cash. Rosie and Herb might not want to ask him to do that, but—"

"I will." Damon took an angry pull from his beer. "I'd have no problem confronting him with the facts of life. He can't go merrily on while Rosie and Herb sink like a stone."

"But they wouldn't be sinking if they had the retirement money. Williams isn't the true villain of this story," Cade said. "Besides, if Rosie and Herb don't want to ask him to sell everything he owns so he can pay them back, then that's all there is to it. We have no right to interfere."

"We certainly don't." Lexi finished off her beer and immediately all three men asked if she needed another. "Thanks, but I'd better not. I'm driving."

"You can stay over," Finn said. "Herb and Rosie wouldn't care."

"I know, but I planned all along to go back to my apartment tonight."

Damon regarded her with a look that was hard to decipher. "You should stay. There are what, four spare bedrooms in this place?"

"What he said." Finn pointed the neck of his bottle in her direction. "We have a lot more to discuss, and it'll go better if you have another beer. We need you to help us figure this out. And Ringo looks mighty comfortable. Stay over."

It made sense. Rosie had asked her to keep these guys from hatching a dramatic plan that would bankrupt all of them. If she left too soon, they could still do that. Yet staying would have consequences when it came to the man sitting across the table from her.

She looked over and found him watching her with amusement. He'd love to have her stay. If she did, sure as the world he'd cook up some scheme so they could be alone. If she were honest with herself, that's what she wanted. "Okay, I'll stay. And I'll have another beer."

Cade smiled. "I'll get it." When he brought her the beer, Ringo gazed up at him with an extremely self-satisfied expression. Cade leaned down and scratched behind the cat's ears. "Traitor."

"He just recognizes a good thing when he sees it," Damon said.

Lexi wouldn't be surprised if Damon had intended that to be a dig at Cade for walking away from her five years ago. At the time he'd told her point-blank that Cade was a damned fool.

Cade didn't linger beside her, and she was grateful for that. Being close to him and knowing what likely would happen later made her heart hammer. She waited until her hands stopped trembling before she picked up the beer. The cold bottle felt great. She wanted to hold it against her cheek, but that would be a little obvious.

She had a hunch Damon might know something about what had happened this morning. Finn was apparently clueless, but Cade had picked up Damon shortly after that last hot kiss this morning. Damon and Cade always had been closer to each other than to Finn. She could picture Cade confiding in Damon and asking him to keep his mouth shut.

"So where are we with this?" Damon glanced around the table. "There's a good chance Rosie and Herb won't allow us to lean on the borrower, and the retirement money won't suddenly reappear, so short of robbing a bank, how can we bail them out?"

Finn started peeling the label from his bottle. "I could sell my business."

"No, you couldn't." She was touched by how quickly Finn offered up the only thing he had. Rosie had been so right about that. "Rosie and Herb would have a fit."

"As well they should," Damon said. "I, on the other hand, could turn on the afterburners and get my current project finished and sold ahead of schedule. If I jump into another one and do that in record time, too, I could end up with a chunk of money to donate to the cause. I can probably get another credit card to tide me over."

"Rosie wouldn't like that any better. You need that income to keep your business going." Lexi was so glad she was here to keep the guys from doing anything heroic but stupid.

"All I have is Hematite." Cade hesitated. "He's not worth a whole lot now because he's never been ridden." He squared his shoulders. "But I could train him and then sell him. He's a fine-looking horse."

Her heart ached to hear him offer the gelding he'd rescued and paid for with his savings. "That can't happen, either. Rosie warned me that you'd all react like this, and she'll be furious if any of you sacrifice to that extent. I'm sure she means it, too. There has to be another way."

Cade's chin jutted. "One thing's for sure. They're not selling the ranch."

"But what if they want to?" Lexi had to put it out there, even if they didn't care to hear it. "What if they're tired of maintaining this big old place and it would be a relief to sell it? Because of the second mortgage they took out, they wouldn't get the full value, but they'd get enough to buy a little house in town."

Three pairs of eyes gazed at her in disbelief.

"Look, you have to put aside what you want, which is to keep this ranch as is so you can make nostalgic visits, and think about what they want. And FYI, none of you have been making very many visits."

Damon let out a breath. "You've got me there, sunshine. I kept meaning to come over more often, but life got in the way."

"Yeah, me, too." Finn's expression was bleak. "When I moved to Seattle, I told myself I'd come back a couple of times a year. I was lucky if I made it once a year."

"Obviously I didn't make it back at all." Cade glanced at Lexi. "I sincerely regret it, too."

"My point is that while it sounds nice and cozy to keep the ranch going, is it fair to expect them to do it so those of you who stayed here have the comfort of knowing it's the way you remembered?"

"No," Cade said. "You're right. And if they want to sell, they should. But this sounds like they have no choice. I want them to have a choice."

"Well said." Damon raised his bottle in Cade's direction. "So if we can come up with a way to raise the money without endangering our own futures, then that gives them the choice. If they don't want to take it, that's up to them."

Lexi glanced at Finn. "You didn't have much money when you moved to Seattle. I never thought to ask how you got the capital for that business. I doubt a bank would have loaned it to you."

"They wouldn't have. I used a crowdfunding campaign."

They all stared at him and then looked at each other.

Cade began to grin. "Is everyone else thinking what I'm thinking?"

"It could be exactly what we need," Damon said. "I can't believe I didn't think of that. Damn it, this could work!"

"Not so fast," Finn said. "You can't just set up an account and ask for money. It needs to be a project with mass appeal. Nobody but the kids who stayed at Thunder Mountain will care whether the Padgetts sell the ranch."

Lexi had figured that, but no mass appeal ideas were coming to her. "What was your hook for the microbrewery?"

"I found a semi-historic building that was scheduled to be demolished. Turned out people were sentimental about it, which helped a lot. I proposed to save it and turn it into a viable business, which would revitalize that area."

Damon looked impressed. "That's brilliant. Unfortunately there's nothing semi-historic about Thunder Mountain Ranch. Judging from the architectural style, I'd say it was built in the fifties."

"Maybe somebody famous lived here," Finn said.

Cade swallowed a mouthful of beer. "If they had, Rosie would have loved telling us about it. I think we're as famous as it gets."

"Then we're in trouble." Finn glanced around the kitchen. "People would donate to revive it as a foster home, but if Rosie and Herb's retirement is gone, they need a decent income producer."

"They'd be okay if they sell, though. There's equity in the place." Lexi wouldn't let the guys forget that option. She didn't want to see that happen, either, but it might be the least stressful outcome for Rosie and Herb.

"They could do a reverse mortgage," Finn said.

Damon pushed back his chair. "Okay, that's another idea, but it doesn't sing to me. They could still end up scrimping their way through their golden years. I like the crowdfunding option, but it needs more brainstorming and my brain's fried."

"Mine, too." Finn stood.

"We'll tackle the subject again tomorrow when we're not so tired." Damon gathered up empty beer bottles and carried them over to the recycling bin in the corner of the kitchen.

"Good idea." Finn threw away the pizza box. "We'll take our stuff down to the cabin and get a good night's sleep. Then we can meet back here for breakfast and talk about it some more."

"You two go ahead." Cade stood, too. "I have something to discuss with Lexi."

"Sure." Damon scrubbed a hand over his face, but not before Lexi caught his grin. "How about we take your cat? You know a cabin's just not complete without a cat."

"If you can pry him off Lexi's lap, then go for it."

"Piece of cake." Damon walked over to where Lexi sat cradling Ringo. "Hey, fur ball, there will be kitty treats and play toys before bedtime down at the cabin. Wanna come with me?"

Cade peered at his friend. "And what kitty treats and play toys would those be?"

"When we stopped to pick up cat food, I bought some kitty yummies, a couple of catnip mice and a feather wand. You must have missed that."

"I do believe I did." Cade shoved back his hat to study Damon. "I thought you were all about dogs. Since when did you become a cat guy?"

"You must not have been paying attention, Gallagher. I've always liked cats." Damon neatly scooped Ringo into his arms. "Especially great ones like this dude. Come on, Ringo. It's you and me, buddy." Damon tucked the purring cat against his shoulder and glanced over at Finn. "You coming, brewmeister?"

"Yep. I hope you got fish flavored, because those usually go over better than chicken."

"I got some of each, just in case."

"Good idea. What brand?" The two men left the kitchen discussing the merits of various kitty treats.

"They've kidnapped your cat." Pulse racing, Lexi pushed back her chair and stood to face the man she hadn't been able to resist since she'd turned sixteen.

"Looked to me like he went willingly." He pulled her slowly into his arms. "How about you?"

"As you probably recall, I've never been interested in telling you no."

He nestled her against his hard body as his green gaze lingered on her mouth. "I'm counting on that."

"But…not here."

"No, not here." He leaned down and brushed her mouth with his. "Let's take a drive."

10

LIKE ANY SENSIBLE cowboy who drove in unpredictable Rocky Mountain weather, Cade kept a couple of blankets tucked behind the passenger seat of his truck. He'd gotten new ones since he and Lexi had been dating. Back then blankets had been for emergencies in the winter and lovemaking in the summer.

"I've never had sex on these," Lexi said once they'd arrived at their old make-out spot and he spread the blankets out in the back of his pickup.

He left his hat on the tailgate and hopped down to gather her close. "Matter of fact, I've never made love to anyone but you in the back of this truck."

She smiled and nestled against him. "Because no other woman would put up with it, I'll bet."

"*No*. Because the back of this truck is…ours."

"Oh, Cade." Her sigh was long and heartfelt.

That tender sound stirred him in ways that he couldn't even begin to identify. The urge to bond with her in a basic, earthy way was so strong—he needed her clothes off *now*. A few clouds had moved in, and the half-moon continued to play hide-and-seek. In the gaps between the clouds, the stars glittered like rhine-stones on a fancy pair of tight jeans. He wanted her stretched out on those blankets, moonlight and star-light gleaming on her skin as he touched every inch of her warm body. After boosting her up to the tailgate, Cade pulled off her boots and tucked them in a corner of the truck bed. He'd always put her boots right there, and he had some superstitious idea that if he followed their pattern, they'd re-create the magic they'd known all those years ago.

She remembered her cues and pulled off her knit shirt. The next move was his. Reaching behind her back, he unhooked her bra and drew it slowly off as he kissed every precious inch he revealed. At last his mouth closed over her nipple, and she clutched his head with a soft moan.

Their lovemaking this morning had been incredible, but he'd missed this, the sweetness of that tight bud against his tongue and the way her breathing changed as he sucked. She was sensitive to this particular caress and sometimes would come with nothing more than his mouth at her breast.

But he longed to touch her in other ways. When he unfastened her jeans and slipped his hand underneath the denim, she parted her thighs and his blood pumped faster. She might have changed her attitude about many things, but in this, she was his Lexi, wanting his touch, wanting his thrusting fingers to bring her pleasure.

As he used his lips and tongue to tease her breast, he stroked her slick heat, causing her to gasp his name. Pushing deeper, he coaxed her up, up, until she surren-dered with the sharp cry that had haunted his dreams.

He felt her climax from his fingers to his toes. He damned near came with her.

But he held back, and, as she drifted down to earth, he stepped away from the truck and took off his clothes. His friends had done him a favor by asking him to bring his cat to the kitchen, because that had given him a chance to stuff a couple of condoms in his pocket. He'd had no guarantee that he'd use them tonight, but having Lexi on the property had been a start.

By the time he climbed up on the tailgate, she'd wiggled out of her jeans and lay waiting for him on the blankets.

He knelt beside her and laid both condoms in her hand. "Hold on to these for later."

"How much later? I need—"

"It's been a long time, Lexi. I didn't get to do all that I wanted to this morning." He smiled at her. She probably couldn't see that in the dark, so he leaned down and nibbled at her mouth. "You're delicious, and I've missed you so much."

"I've missed you, too." She wrapped her hand around his cock. "Don't I get a taste?"

His heart thumped wildly, and he had to swallow before he could speak. "Is that what you want?"

"Yes. Yes, I do."

"I'm...I'm a little out of practice."

"Me, too. So let's practice together."

Excitement threatened to sabotage his control as he made a one-eighty turn to give her what she'd asked for. They'd experimented with this when they'd first discovered sex. While it required a certain amount of coordination, they'd taken that as a challenge and had discovered they liked it. A lot.

She'd said she was out of practice. Had she saved this special pleasure for him? Maybe in her mind, as in his, this also belonged only to them.

And oh, sweet heaven, it was as wonderful as he remembered. As he sipped the tangy juices of her arousal from the soft petals of her secret center, she took his aching cock deep into her hot mouth. Sucking gently, she taunted him with flicks of her tongue and light pressure from her teeth.

He groaned and took his intimate kiss deeper. He used his tongue more aggressively, and as she applied more pressure, so did he. She massaged his balls, and he cupped her firm little ass. Pressing his fingers into her soft skin, he spread her thighs wider, giving him greater access.

His climax hovered, demanding release. Then she lifted her hips at the same moment she took him deep. He sucked hard on her clit as his cock touched the back of her throat. They both came in a blizzard of sensation that was a hundred times, a thousand times, more intense than he remembered.

And as they took all that each of them had to give, a soft rain began to fall on his bare back and the clenching muscles of his buttocks and thighs. Slowly his trembling body grew still, and she relaxed against the blankets. Raindrops gently touched his skin.

He shifted back around so he could gaze into her shadowed face. "It's raining."

"I know."

"Do you want to get into the cab?"

"No. Do you?"

"No. Still got a condom?"

"Yes, but you can't be ready to—"

"Like I said, it's been a long time." He rolled the condom on his stiff cock. He hadn't been this quick to recover since he'd been a teenager. He pushed effortlessly into her orgasm-slick channel and made long, slow love to her while the rain fell in a soothing, steady rhythm.

It ran in rivulets over his back and shoulders and onto her face and breasts. He paused to lick the drops from her nipples, from the hollow of her throat, from her smiling lips.

"I like this," she murmured.

"Me, too." The rain dribbled between his thighs and mingled with her juices until they were both slippery as otters. The squish and slide of their bodies moving together was the most erotic sound he'd ever heard.

He wanted it to go on forever, but his climax edged closer with each thrust. He traced her rain-wet mouth with his tongue. "Can you come?"

"Oh, yes. I'm trying to wait, but—"

"Don't wait." He pumped faster.

"Not waiting." She dug her fingers into his back.

When her hot channel contracted, he drew back once more. Pushing in hard, he surrendered to his body's fierce demands. His cock pulsed within her as she arched upward with a wild cry of release. Gasping, he shoved deeper, wanting…wanting…Lexi. Only Lexi.

As the aftershocks lessened, he rested his forehead against hers. "And I thought this morning was epic."

She stroked his back, her palms slick against his skin. "We've never done it in the rain."

"For good reason." He lifted his head to gaze down at her. "You were still living at your folks' house then. I couldn't take you back there looking like a drowned rat."

"Do I look like one now?"

"Can't tell. Too dark."

"Bet I do." She laughed. "And I don't care. This has been awesome."

"Yeah." He dropped a sweet kiss on her mouth. "It—" A rumble in the distance made whatever he'd been about to say unimportant. "Okay, time to pack up. Rain is one thing. Thunder and lightning is something else."

"I agree."

After rolling away from her, he removed the condom and left it in the truck bed. He'd deal with that later. "Forget your clothes for now." He crawled to the tailgate and jumped down. "I'll carry you back to the cab."

"You don't have to. I can—"

"Come here, Lexi."

"Okay." She crawled to the edge of the tailgate.

He scooped her into his arms and started toward the front of the truck. "You sure are slippery."

"I said I'd walk."

"I like you when you're slippery." Rocks and pine needles bit into the bottoms of his feet, but he ignored the pain as he hurried to the passenger door. "You'd better open it." He angled her so she could reach.

She'd no sooner clutched the door handle than lightning cracked close by. She flung the door open and he dumped her onto the seat.

"You're coming in, too!" She grabbed his arm, and because he was off balance, she managed to pull him partially through the opening.

Rather than stay like that, he crawled the rest of the way in and managed to close the door just before another bolt of lightning slammed down. For a split second everything was bright as day, but then blackness closed in again.

That was the thing about Wyoming. When you drove into the boonies to make out, you'd better have a flashlight because it would be pitch-dark. His was in the glove compartment and there was no way he could open that with both of them tangled up on the passenger side.

Maybe not being able to see had heightened his other senses. The fragrance of sex seemed to fill the cab, and each tentative movement on his part put him in contact with her soft, womanly body. Her skin was still wet, which reminded him of how good she'd felt as he'd eased in and out. In no time at all, he wanted her again.

"Um, Cade?"

"I'm squashing you, I know. I'd turn on the dome light, but the bulb's out and I haven't gotten around to replacing it. Give me a second to figure out the best way to maneuver across the console into the driver's seat."

"I don't mind being squashed. You're not hurting me or anything, but I'm worried that pretty soon you'll put my eye out."

"With what?"

Warm fingers wrapped around his cock. "This."

He started laughing and couldn't seem to stop.

"Now it's jiggling but getting harder."

"I don't doubt it." He gulped for air, but fresh bursts of laughter kept bubbling up. He wondered if a man could have a climax and laugh at the same time. Still chuckling, he reached down and put his hand over hers. "You can let go now. I'll make sure I don't do any damage with my mighty battering ram."

"Or, since I'm holding the second condom in my other hand, I could—"

"You have it?"

"I'd put it down while we had rain sex, but when I started crawling toward you my knee bumped it, so I picked it up. No sense losing it."

"Guess not."

"We made love in this seat once before, remember?"

"I remember everything we ever did together, Lexi. It was snowing."

"Yep. And now it's thundering." She stroked his cock. "Seems a shame to waste a perfectly good erection."

He started laughing again, but the sound of foil tearing sobered him up fast. "You're serious about this."

"Why not?"

"Because I don't know if I can reverse our positions without hurting you. The other time we had it all worked out in advance. I sat down first and then you climbed onto my lap. Now I'm sort of in your lap."

"Trust me."

As she smoothly rolled on the condom, he decided he had no choice. Sometimes a guy had to do what a guy had to do. They went through a few contortions before his bare butt settled into the imitation leather seat, and he hit his funny bone on the dash. But he managed to keep her bruise-free, and that was the main thing.

Well, no, it wasn't. When she straddled his hips, placed her hands on his shoulders and lowered herself onto his waiting cock, *that* was the main thing. At first she went slow enough that he could cup her breasts and play with her nipples. But then she picked up speed.

As her backside slapped his thighs, their ragged breathing drowned out the thunder. Her cries of pleasure and his deep groans muffled the crash of lightning.

As they held each other close while their bodies quivered, he was willing to believe it was snowing outside and their five years apart had been a bad dream.

"The storm's over." She cupped his face in both hands and feathered a kiss over his mouth. "We should head back."

"I don't want to leave. Let's homestead this spot, build a cabin, live here forever."

Her breath caught. "Cade, I—"

"Just kidding." Whatever she'd been about to say, he didn't want to give her a chance to say it. Not tonight. Not when they'd made love in the rain and overpowered the thunder with their cries.

"I knew that." She climbed off his lap with great care and moved to the driver's seat.

"I don't know how to build a cabin, anyway." He opened the glove compartment and took out a trash bag for the condom. "I could get Damon to do it, but he'd probably make me get permits and inspections. I just want to cut down some trees, notch them like Lincoln Logs and put the thing together."

"Yeah, Damon would be all about building to code." She leaned her head back against the seat. "He knows about us, doesn't he?"

No point in denying it. "Does that upset you?"

"Not really. If you move back like you're hinting you might, then everybody will assume we're together unless we tell them different."

"I'm moving back."

"I figured." She sounded amused.

"And not only because of the great sex we just had, smarty-pants."

"I know." She turned her head to look at him, even

though neither of them could see each other very well. "There's Rosie and Herb, and whatever help you can be to them right now. And you love the mountains."

And you, a feeling that goes way beyond sex. But he didn't say that. "Then there's this crazy thing with my relatives. If I'm going to get to know them, I want to do it from here, from my home base. I don't know if that makes any sense now that I've said it out loud. But it's what I want to do."

"It makes a lot of sense," she murmured. "Your roots are *here*, not with some newly discovered branch of your biological tree. You don't want to get pulled off center."

"Exactly!" He reached over and found her hand in the darkness. "Thank you for getting that." He laced his fingers through hers and brought her hand to his mouth. "I really don't want to leave this spot." He kissed her fingers. "I like when it's just you and me, and we can talk like this."

"You're sure it's not because you're dreading those clammy jeans and shirt? Not to mention the damp underwear?"

"Well, there's that." So she didn't want to talk about serious stuff tonight. At least she hadn't mentioned only seeing him when it was convenient. He was pretty sure she'd had as much fun tonight as he had, so chances were she'd find it convenient to see him often.

She squeezed his hand. "Come on, Gallagher. Let's pull on those wet clothes and go back to the ranch."

"And you'll stay in one of the spare rooms, right?"

"I will if you promise to go down to the cabin. This has been perfect, but having sex in one of those spare rooms would feel weird."

"Believe it or not, I agree with you."

"Good." She opened the driver's-side door. "Then let's go find our clothes and put on enough to keep from violating any public decency laws."

"Nobody's going to see us. We could—"

"Sorry, not doing that. We'll inspire enough gossip without being caught driving a county road naked. Get dressed."

"Yes, ma'am." Pulling on his clothes wasn't nearly as much fun as taking them off, and the drive home wasn't remotely comfortable. But he couldn't complain about the way things had turned out. He and Lexi were back together in every way that counted.

He parked the truck next to Lexi's in the circular drive so she could pick up the overnight bag she'd brought to the ranch at the beginning of the crisis with Rosie and hadn't taken home yet. Then he insisted on walking her to the door before taking the path to the cabins. The porch light revealed how bedraggled they both looked.

She grinned at him. "You'd better hope Damon and Finn are asleep, or there will be an interrogation."

"See how easy you have it?"

"But I have to be careful to mop up after myself. I can't leave a trail of water on the hardwood floor, but the cabin floor doesn't matter so much."

"Guess not." He pulled her close, soggy clothes and all. "Before I forget, don't worry about feeding the horses and turning them out in the morning. We'll do it."

"Thanks."

"You're welcome." He ran his fingers through the

damp curls above her ear. "I didn't think I ever wanted you to cut your hair, but I like it short."

She met his gaze. "Good, because it's much easier for me to deal with when I'm traveling, so I plan to keep it this way for a while."

He caught the challenging light in her eyes. "Did I say something wrong?"

Sighing, she relaxed against him. "No. I'm glad you like my hair short, because even if you didn't, I wouldn't grow it long just to please you."

That startled him. "Is that what you did before? Leave it long because I liked it that way?"

"I'm afraid so. Everything I did was based on how you'd react, what would make you happy."

"Wow, Lexi. I had no idea." Gradually he was beginning to understand the problem, and it might be more complex than he'd thought.

"You never asked that of me. I just automatically adjusted my behavior to accommodate you, and you seemed happy to be in charge."

He was flabbergasted. "I thought you wanted me to be in charge!"

"Maybe I did, but I don't anymore." She touched his cheek. "When you ordered me to the end of the tailgate so you could carry me to the cab, I almost refused."

He groaned. "I didn't mean to *order* you, but I was scared about the lightning. If anything happened to you…" He hugged her close. "We'll work on it, Lexi. This is important."

"Uh-huh." She sniffed.

He tipped her chin up. "Are you crying?"

"No. Yes. It's been…a very long day."

"It has." He brushed his thumbs across her cheeks. "Go get some rest."

Her laugh was watery. "Was that an order?"

He gazed at her and replayed what he'd just said. "I guess you could call it that. Bad habit." He took a deep breath. "I don't know how tomorrow will go, and I'm sure you'll want to get back to your apartment tomorrow night."

"Yes."

"So, I was wondering… Would it be convenient if I came to see you there?"

She smiled. "It would."

"Thank God." He gave her a deep kiss with lots of tongue, and then he released her, turned away and walked to the cabin without looking back. At their make-out spot he'd imagined that they'd never been apart.

But that kind of thinking would get him in trouble. They had been apart, and they'd both changed from the people they'd been five years ago. Apparently he'd been a typical arrogant male expecting her to go along with whatever, and she hadn't been strong enough yet to tell him to go to hell. But now she was.

That made it critical for him to figure out who she was now, and who he was. He had a hunch that of the two of them, she'd made the most progress. She might not wait for him to catch up.

Obviously the sex was still great, but he was beginning to understand that he had some things to learn and some attitudes to change. He wasn't sure how good he was at that kind of thing. If he couldn't master it, he was headed for heartbreak.

11

LEXI HAD LEFT the bedroom window open, so she was awakened by the sound of male laughter drifting in. The pale glow of early morning told her the sun was barely up, but the Brotherhood seemed to be awake and doing their cowboy thing.

A gate creaked and the slap of a hand against a horse's rump was followed by the hoofbeats of several horses trotting into the pasture. Comments were tossed back and forth. She couldn't make out the words, but more laughter followed.

After getting out of bed, she went to the window and pulled back the curtain. She had a clear view of the pasture from here, and the scene was pure female fantasy. As the horses cavorted in the grass, which sparkled with dew, three broad-shouldered cowboys leaned against the fence to watch them.

Cade was on the left. She'd know those cute buns anywhere. Damon, who was more muscular than Finn, was in the middle. Finn might not have Damon's bulk, but he possessed a lean appeal that women had always found sexy. Damon and Finn must have discovered the old straw cowboy hats Herb relegated to the barn after Rosie had pronounced them too disreputable to wear in public.

Lined up along the fence, hats tipped back and jeans stretched as they each propped a booted foot on the bottom rail, the Thunder Mountain Brotherhood provided a visual treat that any woman would have appreciated. Too bad she was the only one around to enjoy it.

Pushing away from the fence, they turned and started toward the house, still talking and joking. Finn said something that made the other two laugh. When Cade's grin flashed, Lexi caught her breath. The boy who'd captured her heart at sixteen had become a man to be reckoned with. But then, she'd become a woman to be reckoned with. The future would be interesting, indeed.

She left the window and grabbed a change of clothes, ducking into the bathroom down the hall. By the time she'd showered and dressed, the smell of coffee brewing and the murmur of voices told her the guys were cooking breakfast. She recognized Cade's soft chuckle.

Then she smelled biscuits baking and decided having three handsome cowboys cook her breakfast was a great way to begin the day. She'd started out of her bedroom when the house's landline rang in the kitchen. She quickened her step. Maybe there was news about Rosie.

As she entered the kitchen, Finn was on the phone talking earnestly. Cade glanced her way immediately and smiled, but he didn't say anything, as if he didn't want to miss a single word of Finn's conversation.

Damon stood by the stove. Bacon sizzled in one frying pan and eggs cooked in another, but Damon wasn't paying attention to any of it. His spatula was motionless in his hand as he listened to Finn.

"Yeah, I'll tell them. It's very good news. Excellent news. We'll see you soon. Bye, Dad." He hung up the phone and turned, his blue eyes glowing with excitement. "They want to keep her longer for observation and do some more tests, but the preliminary evaluation is that it wasn't a heart attack."

"Yee-haw! Conga line!" Damon began dancing around the kitchen table and punching his spatula in the air as he chanted out the beat. "Show some spirit, Brotherhood!"

Laughing, Cade and Finn jumped in behind him. Finn glanced at Lexi. "Are you dancing or what?"

"I'm dancing, I'm dancing!" Apparently for the moment, she was one of the guys, and as they celebrated Rosie's good news together, she was ridiculously happy to be included.

No telling how long the parade would have continued if Damon hadn't yelled "Shit!" and dashed for the stove. "Food's starting to burn," he announced. "Grab plates and silverware. Breakfast is happening."

They gathered around the table with their plates of slightly overdone bacon and scrambled eggs. Finn refilled everyone's coffee mug and got a fourth one out of the cupboard for Lexi.

She thanked him for the coffee and sat down, once again choosing a seat across from Cade. Somebody was missing from the group, and finally she figured out who that was. "Where's Ringo?"

"Sleeping it off." Cade chuckled as he dug into his scrambled eggs. "Apparently they wore him out playing with him. He's catching z's on my bed with his mice between his paws."

"Yeah, wanna see?" Damon pulled out his phone and showed her a picture.

"Aww. He looks like a happy guy."

Cade sighed and shook his head. "If he were any happier, he'd be levitating. Harrison, I can't believe you now have a picture of my cat on your phone. What the hell?"

"It's cute. I might make it my screen saver." He popped a piece of crisp bacon in his mouth and crunched down.

"I already did." Finn passed Lexi his phone. "This is from last night when he was playing with the feather wand. That cat can jump, too. He—"

"Hey, losers." Cade cradled his coffee mug. "Promise me that when you get home, you'll find a shelter and adopt a kitty-cat, okay?"

"Wouldn't work for me." Damon continued to eat. "I move too often, and I don't think that's fair to the cat. It's a disadvantage of my job, because I love animals. I miss that about living here. Besides the horses, we always had dogs and cats."

"I had a dog and a cat," Finn said. "Alison got custody."

Cade frowned. "That sucks."

"No, she should have them." He forked up more eggs. "As she pointed out, I work all the time. I didn't spend enough time with them."

Lexi was no psychologist, but it didn't take an expert to see that both guys were working themselves to the bone and ignoring their emotional needs. She knew enough of their history to understand why they'd do that. They were determined to succeed.

But no wonder they'd gone crazy over Ringo. During the rest of the meal they couldn't resist showing her all the pictures they'd taken, and there were a bunch. "I have to agree with Cade," she said. "You both need animals in your life."

"Not feasible," Damon said.

"What if you adopt two cats so that when you move them they'll have each other to provide stability?"

Damon slowly nodded. "I'll think about that. It might work. Thanks."

"And Finn, you could do the same thing, and then you wouldn't feel so guilty when you're not there all the time."

"Yeah, two cats." Finn smiled. "Good concept. I like it."

Damon stood and started collecting plates. "Now that we have the cat issue under control, we should get over to the hospital. Rosie will wonder where the hell we are."

He'd been the first to begin tidying up last night, too. Lexi had forgotten that he was a neat freak after being forced to live in a pigsty of a house until he'd run away from home at twelve. She finished her coffee and pushed back her chair. "What about our brainstorming?"

Damon stopped loading the dishwasher. "Right. We need to do that. But we should get to the hospital and celebrate Rosie's good news with her. How about we brainstorm on the way? We can put our cell phones on speaker."

"That works." Lexi glanced at Finn. "Are you riding with me?"

"That would be great." He dumped the coffee grounds in the garbage. "But I feel like we're putting you out. Maybe we should just rent a car today."

"I don't mind taking you."

Damon finished loading the dishwasher and turned it on. "Yeah, but he'll need a ride back here later on. Is it too much trouble?"

"Not really." She avoided looking at Cade, but the unspoken thoughts zipped between them, anyway. Would she stay again so they could make love tonight? *Yes.* Were they moving too fast? *Maybe.*

"That's good." Damon turned on the dishwasher. "Once Rosie's home, transportation won't be an issue. Plus Rosie and Herb's truck will be here if we need it."

That would put a limit on how many nights she stayed at the ranch, which was probably a good thing. When Rosie came home, she'd return to her apartment. If Cade spent the night there, and he quite likely would, the dynamic would be different. In subtle ways, the back of the truck tied them to their past when they needed to focus on a different kind of future.

She glanced around the kitchen to see if anything more needed to be done, but the guys seemed to have it covered. Cade handled the final chore of wiping down the table and the counters. She gave Rosie a mental salute for doing such a good job teaching her boys to clean up after themselves. Damon hadn't needed much coaxing, but most of the others had required guidance.

Cade finished and rinsed the dishrag under the kitchen faucet. "I just thought of something. If Mom didn't have a heart attack, then what happened? Did Dad say?"

"He did." Finn leaned against the counter. "It's called broken heart syndrome."

Cade turned to stare at him. "What the hell is *that*?"

"It sounds bogus to me." Damon's chin jutted. "Like

they don't know what's wrong so they make something up."

"This could be legit," Finn said. "The doc explained to Dad that it's a reaction to stress that mostly hits women in Mom's age bracket. It looks and feels like a heart attack, and it can be serious if someone's not very healthy to begin with. But Mom could be home in a couple of days."

"That's great that she'll be home so soon." Cade massaged the back of his neck and gazed at his companions. "But if she has a broken heart, I think we all know why."

Damon nodded. "The prospect of selling the ranch."

"Right. So regardless of her claim that they can just sell and everything will be hunky-dory, it won't be. It'll break her heart."

Finn took a deep breath. "Well, that's not acceptable. Last night we talked about wanting to give them a choice about whether to sell or not. If you ask me, selling is no longer an option."

"I have to agree." Lexi saw the light of battle in their eyes. "But the solution can't jeopardize any of you, because that would also break her heart."

"Shit." Damon took off his battered straw hat and ran his fingers through his sun-streaked hair. "We could go around to their friends and get donations, which I'd do in a heartbeat, but they'd hate that, too."

"Yeah, they would." Cade looked at Finn. "I keep coming back to that crazy crowdfunding idea, but damned if I know how we can make that work."

"I like the concept, too," Lexi said. "We just have to come up with a worthwhile concept that will get people excited."

Damon gave her a dark look. "Not easy."

She didn't flinch. "Not impossible."

"No, it's not." Cade sent her a quick smile of encouragement. "We have a few days to put together a plan. Give a shout-out if you get any ideas on the drive in, and tonight we'll toss it all out there and see what happens."

Damon straightened. "Are we ready to roll?"

"Give me a sec." Lexi headed to her room. Knowing she would be coming back here tonight meant she could leave her damp jeans draped over the shower curtain rod in the bathroom and her shirt and undies on hangers hooked on the closet doorknob.

Grabbing her purse from the dresser, she started digging her keys out. She ran smack into Cade in the doorway.

His arms came around her. "In a hurry?"

She looked into green eyes filled with the tender light that never failed to get her blood pumping. He'd left his hat somewhere else, so he clearly had a plan. "Cade, they're waiting for us."

"No, they're not. I loaned them my truck. I'm riding with you."

She had a sudden embarrassing image of what they'd done in his truck last night.

"Don't worry. I went over it with a fine-tooth comb before I went to bed. I even hung the wet blankets in an empty stall to dry."

"Thank you."

"You're welcome."

"But we have to leave. Otherwise they'll wonder what's keeping us."

He grinned. "Oh, they'll know what's keeping us. Finn has caught on."

"Even more reason! I don't want them thinking that we're—"

"Just a couple of minutes. I desperately need to kiss you. I feel like I'm gonna explode."

She relented. "Can't have that." Cupping the back of his head, she pulled him down and angled her mouth over his.

He moaned softly and pulled her in tight. His body was rock hard, especially the part she'd become reacquainted with yesterday. His tongue sought the recesses of her mouth with deliberate intent. He was frustrated and obviously wanted her to share that frustration.

That didn't take long. In no time she matched him moan for moan, and when he slipped his hand under her T-shirt to unhook her bra, she didn't stop him. She should have. This was crazy, but his hands... How she loved the way he stroked her bare breasts until they ached for his kiss. Wrenching his mouth from hers, he pushed up her shirt and leaned down to give her what she longed for.

Tugging at her nipple with his lips and tongue, he rubbed the crotch of her jeans with firm pressure. They'd spent many hours making out in his truck, and he knew all the ways to give her pleasure even with their clothes mostly on.

With a quick gasp, she came, soaking her panties and dampening her jeans. He drew back and kissed her firmly on the mouth before stepping away. "That's to tide us over until tonight."

"I..." She dragged in a breath. "I...need to change."

"Go ahead." He backed toward the door. "I'll wait out by your truck. I'm in control now, but I can't promise anything if you strip off your jeans."

She glanced at the hard ridge pushing at his fly. "What about you?"

"I've had lots of practice at decompressing. It'll be gone by the time you walk out the door." He left.

This romance was creating laundry issues, but she'd worry about that later. After taking her third and last pair of jeans and panties from her little suitcase, she quickly changed and reapplied her lipstick. As she glimpsed her reflection in the mirror, she saw a woman dazed by the swiftness with which this man could seduce her.

Because that was exactly what he'd done. He'd known from the moment he sent his friends off in his truck that he'd use the time to give her an orgasm. He'd never intended to stop with a kiss. In the back of her mind, she'd known that, and the knowledge had excited her.

She'd always loved his boldness. It was part of what drew her and made him the sexiest man she'd ever met. It was also why he'd so easily claimed her complete attention when they'd been younger. He'd given her pleasure that rivaled anything her romantic soul could imagine.

Like this. She'd been on her way out the door with not a single thought of sex on her mind. In nothing flat he'd ignited her passion and given her a climax. That was talent. Should she embrace it or run like the wind? The jury was still out.

Or maybe not. As she closed the front door and walked out on the porch, there was her cowboy leaning against the front fender of her truck looking adorably cocky. His hat shaded his eyes, but not his wide grin.

He'd managed to provide her with a special moment this morning and obviously he was quite proud of himself.

She couldn't help laughing. "You think you're pretty clever, don't you?"

"Yes, ma'am." He pushed away from the fender, opened the driver's-side door and offered his hand to help her in.

"Do you want to drive?" The minute the words were out of her mouth, she knew exactly where they'd come from—the woman she'd been five years ago. *Damn it.* There was the hidden danger of hanging out with Cade. She would *not* revert to the overly accommodating and dependent person she'd been five years ago, even if that meant pushing him away.

He gazed at her as if considering the question. "No, I don't."

"Okay." She thought about that as he helped her in. Then she tried to remember if she'd ever driven him anywhere. After they were on their way down the road, she asked him.

He shrugged. "I don't know. Probably."

"I can't think of when it would have been. You always liked to take your truck."

"Well, duh. You had that little car back then. Couldn't make out in that thing. And you didn't want to do it on the ground on account of snakes."

His response was logical. Driving somewhere private had been a high priority. He'd lived at the ranch, and she'd lived with her folks. As for a blanket on the ground, the possibility of a snake arriving in the middle of the action did sort of freak her out. "I have a truck now."

"I see that. Nice truck."

"We could take it tonight."

He hesitated. "You got blankets?"

"Of course! You don't go on the road in the winter without blankets, so I just leave them in here all the time."

"Have you ever—"

"No. I've never had truck-bed sex with anyone but you."

"Then how do you know if it's comfortable back there? Mine has a liner."

"So does mine. And I don't know if it's comfortable to lie on or not, but maybe it's time to test it out."

He laughed. "I'm thinking this is a test in more ways than one. You want to know if I can handle having you drive me out to our make-out spot and back in your vehicle or if that would somehow affect my manly pride."

"Would it?"

"Lexi, if you're offering to use your truck and your gas to ferry me out into the boonies so I can give you a screaming orgasm, that's not an ego buster. It's an ego booster. In other words, I'd be honored."

Damn, he was turning her on with that talk. "I don't scream."

"It'll be a whole new venue. This time you just might."

12

CADE THOUGHT THAT had gone well. When she'd asked if he wanted to drive to the hospital, he'd been a whisker away from saying yes. Just in time he'd caught something in her expression that told him yes was not the right answer. But it was the perfect answer to her question about taking the truck tonight.

She was absolutely right that he'd never ridden with her. He'd tried to make it sound like he hadn't noticed one way or the other, but the minute he'd climbed into the passenger seat, he'd felt weird. Looking to his left to see her must be what tourists felt like when driving in England.

He wasn't that way with other people, though. *Other guys*, a little voice reminded him. Humbling though it was, he had to acknowledge that he had a hang-up about being driven by a woman. His jerk of a dad had always insisted on driving, and he'd taken the truck when he'd left. After that, Cade and his mom had depended on the kindness of neighbors when they'd needed to go somewhere.

Lexi had the pedal to the metal. He glanced at the

speedometer and saw she was going about five miles over. "Trying to catch those old boys?"

"I wouldn't mind." She glanced at him. "Do I make you nervous?"

He lied. "No."

"I don't believe you. You have a death grip on your knees. You're denting the denim."

Instantly he relaxed his hands. "This is embarrassing. I'm evolved. I support gender equality."

"Except in a moving vehicle." She sounded amused rather than ticked off.

"There, too! At least intellectually."

"Then this is good practice for you. It'll allow your emotions to catch up with your brain."

"Absolutely. I'll give up driving completely if you're willing to chauffeur me around." Actually that didn't sound like a bad plan.

"Nice try, but I'm not that dedicated to your transformation."

"It was just a thought." As she passed a slow-moving RV, he caught himself gripping his knees again and dug his phone out of his pocket to distract himself. "I should probably text Molly back."

"She texted you?"

"Yeah, this morning, asking if I'd be at the hospital because she wanted to bring me something."

"She's a nice person."

"Seems like it." He sent the text saying he was heading there now and would be there a good part of the day.

"She got me a gig over at the Last Chance the middle of July."

"Oh, yeah?" The reality of being connected to that family hadn't really sunk in. Lexi would be driving over to the ranch where three of his cousins lived. *Amazing.*

"They have a summer program for disadvantaged boys, and they want me to give a riding clinic for them. Want to come along?"

His chest tightened. "Um, I don't know. I'm not sure what I'll be doing at that point."

"I know, but it's only for a couple of days. You don't have to decide now, but I'm sure they'd love to meet you."

"And I want to meet them, too. Eventually." He thought some time should go by before he went charging over there. Maybe weeks, maybe months. The appropriate amount of time wasn't clear in his mind, but mid-July might be too soon.

"Okay." She sounded a little deflated.

"Look, do you *want* me to come with you? For moral support?"

She hesitated. "Yes."

"In that case, I'll go unless I have a job I can't leave or something critical comes up. Like I said, the future's kind of uncertain with the ranch in trouble."

"I understand. But it'll be great if you can go." Her voice had a happy little lilt to it.

Apparently she really had wanted him to go over to Jackson Hole with her. Maybe the Chances intimidated her, too. *Too?* Damn it, was *he* intimidated? The tension in his gut told him the answer. *Well, hell.*

Coming back to Thunder Mountain Ranch was turning out to be an educational experience. In less than two days he'd learned that he was prejudiced against riding with a woman driver and that being instantly related to a powerful family made his stomach hurt.

Finding out these things wasn't particularly pleasant, especially because he considered himself a guy who had his act together.

On the plus side, Lexi wanted to have sex with him as much, and maybe more, than she had before he'd left. He was fairly sure she still loved him, although she hadn't said it. He hadn't said it, either, but it was the only word to describe how he felt.

They were in early days. They'd get to the love talk, and then the marriage talk. He and Lexi needed to be married. He hadn't been ready to make that commitment before, but now he was and it would happen. That was something to hold on to as he dealt with everything else, including whatever happened with the ranch.

She glanced over at him. "You look as if you're relaxing a bit, cowboy."

"I am." Sure enough, he wasn't gripping his knees. His hands rested on his thighs and the tension had left his stomach. He wondered if she'd want to get married in a church or at Thunder Mountain. Better not ask that yet, since he hadn't even declared his love, let alone proposed.

If the ranch no longer belonged to the Padgetts when they were ready to get married, that would suck. "I guess we should be brainstorming this crowdfunding plan some more."

"We should. Any ideas?"

"Not specifically, but the whole thing is brilliant— first to think of raising money that way, and second to figure out what would appeal to people so they'd donate to the cause. Do you suppose Finn came up with all of that by himself?"

"Maybe. He's pretty smart."

"No doubt, but I didn't hear him throwing out concepts right and left for how we could use the idea to save the ranch." He pulled out his phone. "I'm going to ask him."

Finn answered immediately. "Let me guess. You're just now leaving the ranch."

"Smart-ass. We might even beat you there. Listen, did you have anybody working with you on the crowd-funding campaign or was that all you?"

"You mean Chelsea?"

"Who's Chelsea?"

"Chelsea Trask. I met her in line at a coffee shop right after I got to Seattle."

"Hang on a minute. Let me put you on speaker so Lexi can hear this." He looked over at Lexi. "Chelsea Trask. Met her in a coffee shop. This could be the answer to all our problems." Then he pushed the speaker icon. "Okay, go ahead."

"Like I said, Chelsea suggested the crowdfunding idea and agreed to work with me for a percentage of the profits. She's the one who told me to buy the old building and appeal to people's nostalgia about saving it."

"So is she making money from O'Roarke's, then?"

"Oh, yeah. She gets a check every month."

"We need her."

"You mean here in Sheridan? I don't know if that's—"

"She doesn't have to come here in person, but maybe a conference call, or Skype, something so we can lay out our situation and see if she has any ideas. If she'll take the same deal, a percentage of the profits, great. If she wants a fee, then we'll have to see what we can do."

On the other end, Finn cleared his throat. "I guess she'd have to know I'm involved."

"Hell, yes, she'd have to know. I thought you'd be the one to contact her."

"Unfortunately, I'm not her favorite person."

Cade exchanged a look with Lexi. "Why not?"

"Apparently she's always had feelings for me, so after the divorce, she was hoping we'd get together. But I said I needed to concentrate on the business, and she…told me off."

"Oh." Cade's shining hopes began to sink.

"That's why I didn't mention her before. You could try contacting her and pretend you've never heard of me, but she knows too much. That first meeting lasted a couple of hours, and I told her all about Thunder Mountain Ranch. I actually think that's one of the reasons she wanted to help me."

Cade massaged the bridge of his nose. "Remind me how Alison fits into this scenario. I'm confused about the time frame."

"I met her later on. It was lust at first sight, and we flew to Vegas and got married within two months of our first date. Two years later, she asked for a divorce."

"I see this is complicated. We'll have to come up with a strategy. See you at the hospital, bro. Oh, wait. What's our story when we get there? Rosie knows that we know."

Damon's voice came through the speaker. "We tell her that we promise not to put ourselves in jeopardy, but we're working on a solution. Which we are."

"Sounds good. See you there." Cade disconnected the call. "Damn. I thought we had a good resource. Why the hell didn't O'Roarke marry *her*?"

"Because he was thinking with his—"

"Don't say it." Cade held up a hand. "We all do that.

I do that. Who do you think's been in charge ever since I showed up at the ranch the other night? Not my logical brain, I can tell you that."

She laughed. "Then you know why Finn married Alison instead of Chelsea."

"Yes, but he had a second chance, and he blew that one, too!"

"Finn doesn't know what he wants."

"That's obvious, but somehow we have to get Chelsea to help us, regardless of how O'Roarke has screwed up the dynamic."

"I think she will," Lexi said softly.

"You do?" Cade decided there were advantages to being the passenger. He didn't have to pay attention to the road, which left him free to admire the cute tilt of her nose and the graceful curve of her throat. "Why?"

"She loves him."

"I'm not getting that. I think she's gone from loving to loathing without passing Go or collecting two hundred dollars."

Lexi smiled, which created the small dimple he loved so much and which he didn't often get a chance to observe so well. He would kiss that dimple, but she might drive right off the road. "What's so funny?"

"Loving and loathing are two sides of the same coin," she said. "If she cared enough to tell him off, she might still love him. And Finn desperately needs someone to love him."

"Don't we all."

She swallowed. "Yes, we do."

His chest grew warm, and the words rose up, ready to be said. "Lexi, I—"

"Not now. Not when I'm driving in traffic and I can't look into your eyes."

He was stunned into silence. His heart thumped heavily in his chest as he bit back what he'd been about to say. She was right, once again. This was not the time or place.

Even reaching for her hand was dicey because her truck was a stick shift, and the last thing he wanted was to distract her and cause a problem. But he'd get another chance. Unlike O'Roarke, he knew what he wanted.

They rode the rest of the way without talking, but her color was high and he had fun imagining her thoughts. He wondered what kind of ring she'd want. Unlike some guys, he didn't have an heirloom to pass down. He'd have to get something from a store or online.

He wasn't crazy about the online option, but if she wanted an antique, that might be the only way to find it. They'd never talked about rings because the minute he'd realized she wanted a proposal, he'd bolted. He was damned lucky that she hadn't ended up with some other guy.

His truck was in the hospital parking lot, and Lexi let out with a very unladylike swear word when she spotted it. "I was speeding, but Damon must have been *really* speeding."

Cade widened his eyes in mock surprise. "You think?"

"I would have beaten him if I hadn't been worried about scaring you, this being your first trip with a lady driver and all."

"Thanks for being gentle with me." The charged moment when he'd been about to say the right thing at the wrong time had been replaced with their usual irreverent banter, which was fine with him.

"Oh, stuff it, Gallagher. Let's go see Rosie."

Smiling, he walked beside her into the hospital. Life with Lexi would be a constant adventure. He was impatient to make their connection official, but that probably should wait until Rosie was home again and healthy. Then again, Rosie had always wanted them to end up together, and knowing they were engaged might very well speed her recovery.

The hallway outside Rosie's room was empty. Cade guessed that Herb had already let everyone know that Rosie hadn't had a heart attack. The only people in the room were Herb, Damon and Finn.

Herb looked a thousand times better. He'd shaved and changed clothes, plus the terror had faded from his eyes. Cade was glad of that. He wasn't ready for either one of these excellent people to go into a decline.

Rosie seemed much perkier, although he still didn't like seeing her lying in a hospital bed surrounded by machines. She beamed when Cade walked in with Lexi. "There you are! Damon and Finn seem to think you two are back together. Is that right?"

Lexi went over to the bed and perched on the edge while she leaned down and gave Rosie a kiss on the cheek. "I don't hate him, if that's what you mean."

"And I consider that progress." Cade hung back so Lexi could have her time with Rosie.

"Oh, it's progress, all right!" Rosie grinned at him. "You should have heard her curse your name five years ago. With the help of her girlfriends she cursed you in three languages."

"Impressive." After hearing Lexi say that love and hate were two sides of the same coin, that didn't bother him a bit. If she'd gone to all that trouble, deep love was there along with her understandable fury when he'd walked away.

"It was." Rosie was quiet for a moment. Then she took a deep breath and surveyed the group. "I guess you all know about our financial issues."

"We do," Cade said gently. "Lexi explained it."

"And I'm grateful for that. I wasn't looking forward to telling you. The thing is, Herb and I had a chance to talk last night, and we're agreed that it might be time to hang it up. We had a good run, and if that's all she wrote, so be it."

Cade exchanged a look with Damon and Finn. "Maybe so, but we want to see if we can come up with some options. We might as well try, right?"

"That's my feeling," Damon said. "We just need to check out a few things."

Rosie's expression was stern. "But no heroics. Is that understood?"

Damon nodded. "Understood. We—" He stopped talking and glanced toward the doorway where Molly had appeared, a package clutched to her chest. "Hey, Molly. What's up?"

"She has something for me." Cade walked toward her, still unable to believe he had a cousin. No, several cousins.

"Sorry to interrupt." She held out the package. "But I wanted you to have these."

"Come on in, Molly," Herb said.

"Thanks, but I can't." She straightened her large tortoiseshell glasses. "I have an interview at the college. But thanks for calling with the good news this morning. I'm so glad you're doing better, Rosie."

"You and me both." Rosie smiled at her. "Good luck with your interview. They'd be nuts not to hire you."

"Fingers crossed. See you all later!" She whisked out the door and down the hall, heels tapping on the bare floor.

Cade looked at the package wrapped in plain brown paper. It felt like a book, a fairly large one, the kind people put on coffee tables.

Damon sauntered over. "Are you going to open it or drive us all crazy?"

"He doesn't have to if he doesn't want to," Finn said.

"No, it's okay." He took off the wrapping and handed it to Damon. "Hold this."

"As you wish, my liege."

"Bite me, Harrison." Cade had opened it upside down, and all he could see was a plain black binding. The package turned out to be two books, and when he flipped them over, he sucked in a breath. Gallagher Family Tree was embossed in gold on the front of the first book. The second one was identical, except it was for the Chance family.

"Wow, that's cool." Damon peered over his shoulder. "Do you suppose you're in there?"

"Guess so." He opened the front cover and on the inside page Molly had written, "To Cade—Welcome to the family. Love, Molly." His throat tightened and he was terrified that he might lose it. He hadn't cried in fifteen years and damned if he'd do it now, especially in front of everybody.

He shoved the books at Damon. "I left something in the truck. Be right back." And he bolted out the door.

When he got to the parking lot, his eyes were damp and he realized he couldn't have come out here to grab something from either truck. Damon had his keys and Lexi had hers.

Because she was smart enough to realize that, he wasn't surprised to hear her voice.

"You'll need a key."

He swiped at his eyes before turning to face her. He didn't know what to say, how to explain.

Apparently he didn't have to. Without a word, she came over and wrapped her arms around him.

With a groan he pulled her close and rested his cheek against her soft curls.

She hugged him tight. "It's a lot to take in."

"Yeah." And he held on to her until the knot in his chest loosened and he could breathe. "You know what I keep thinking?"

"What?"

"If my mom had let herself reconnect with her people, she'd be alive."

"Oh, Cade." She hugged him tighter. "I don't think she was strong enough to face them."

"Guess not."

"But you are."

"I hope so." The prospect still made his stomach hurt. "I have to admit I'm real nervous about meeting all of them."

"But you will meet them, and it'll be great."

"Yeah." He knew she expected that of him, but he wasn't sure if he could live up to those expectations. Taking a deep breath, he lifted his head and looked around to see if anyone else had come out, like Damon, for instance, with the keys to Cade's truck. He hadn't, thank God.

She gazed up at him. "Better?"

"Yes. Thanks." He hesitated. "I didn't have anything to come out here for."

"I know. We all know."

"Damned embarrassing."

"I saw what she wrote. I would have been worried if you hadn't reacted like this. Why do you suppose she delivered it and hurried off?"

"She had an interview."

"Nice timing, don't you think?"

He stared at her. "So she's as jacked up about this discovery as I am?"

"Maybe not quite as much or in the same way, but I can tell that meeting you has touched her deeply. She's really big on family, which makes this discovery precious to her."

"I don't know why. She's knee-deep in relatives. What's so special about one more?"

Lexi smiled. "You were the boy who went missing, the little lamb who got lost, the calf who strayed from the herd, the—"

"Okay, okay, I get it." She'd made him laugh, which he'd sorely needed. He'd been taking himself way too seriously. "We'd better get back in there. We have work to do."

"Like what?"

"We need to gang up on Finn so he'll call Chelsea and grovel."

13

"OKAY, BUT I'M NOT groveling in front of you guys."
Finn pushed back his chair. They'd all gathered in the
hospital's dining area for lunch, including Herb. They'd
brought him in on the discussion at Lexi's insistence.
She'd seen no point in bothering Chelsea if Herb and
Rosie would nix the idea.

Herb, it turned out, thought crowdfunding was a
brilliant concept. He'd understood the significance of
Rosie's broken heart syndrome and knew that selling
the ranch wasn't a good option. Herb's excitement about
getting Chelsea on board had sealed the deal for Finn.

He pulled out his phone. "Just warning you, she
might not answer my call."

"One way to find out," Damon said.

"See you guys in a few." Finn walked away.

"What if she doesn't answer?" Herb asked the group
at the table.

"I could be wrong," Lexi said, "but if she's cared for
him all this time, I think she'll answer."

Cade leaned back in his chair and adjusted the tilt of
his Stetson. "I hope he doesn't louse it up."

"Me, too." Damon polished off his coffee. "Sounds as if he flat out told her his business takes precedence over everything. That's brutal."

"Maybe for him it does," Lexi said.

Damon sighed. "It probably does, and I get that. He never should have married Alison, and I don't blame him for not wanting to hook up with someone, knowing it could be the same story, with him working all the time and her complaining about it. But you can put it more diplomatically, like, 'I fantasize about a day when I can spend time with a terrific woman like you. I'll probably regret this decision for the rest of my life.' Something like that."

Cade grinned. "I'm guessing you've delivered that line a time or two."

"Sure." Damon shrugged. "I'm in no position to settle down, either. If Lexi's two-cat plan works out, then I'll have friendly faces to greet me when I walk in the door. That's all I need."

"Here comes Finn," Cade said. "He looks kind of wrecked."

Lexi mentally crossed her fingers and prayed her instincts were right about a woman she'd never met.

Finn sank down onto a chair and took a deep breath. He did look wrecked. After taking off the old straw cowboy hat he'd continued to wear all day, he ran his fingers through his coal-black hair. Then he repositioned the hat. "She's going to talk to us on Skype tonight at four her time, which will be five ours. And she's not charging us for the initial consultation."

"Yee-haw!" Damon clapped him on the back. "Congratulations, O'Roarke. I'd buy you a drink, but they don't serve beer in this establishment."

Finn gave him a tired smile. "Speaking of that, we're stopping to pick up beer on the way home and I'm choosing it."

"And you're not paying," Cade said. "Harrison and I are treating you to whatever fancy-ass beer you want, bro." Then he looked over at Herb. "We'll need to borrow your computer, and I hope to hell you have Skype on it."

"We do. Rosie's started using it a little bit." Herb paused to glance at everyone. "I think it's time to tell her what's up."

"So do I," Lexi said. "Since Chelsea's agreed to help, then Rosie should know what's going on."

Cade nodded. "Let's go tell her. If she has some big objection to the idea, then Finn can cancel the Skype call with Chelsea."

"I'd better not have to cancel." Finn gave them all a dark look. "That wasn't an easy conversation to have, FYI. She made it clear she was only helping because she's heard me rave about my life at Thunder Mountain and she admires Rosie and Herb."

Herb smiled. "That's nice to hear."

"She also claimed to be in shock that I was calling her from Wyoming. She asked if I wanted her to drive past O'Roarke's to see if it was still standing without me being there."

Cade gave him a look of sympathy. "Any name-calling?"

"Not this time. Oh, wait. When she answered, she said, 'If it isn't the anal control freak.' So I guess that counts."

"Here's an idea," Damon said. "When we Skype with her tonight, you just stay in the background."

Cade shook his head. "That's the wrong approach. We don't want him to come off as a coward who's afraid to face her."

"I agree with Cade." Lexi was eager to meet this woman, even if she'd only be an image on a computer screen.

"Wish I could be there," Herb said, "but I don't feel right leaving Rosie." His phone chimed. "And there she is." He answered the phone. "You bet. We're on our way." He disconnected and stood. "The doc's there. She has the rest of the test results."

Thirty minutes later, Rosie's doctor had left the room and Rosie glanced over at the case of Baileys in the corner. "Now that it's official that I don't have heart disease, seems like we ought to bust out some of that booze and have a party."

"No, that's for you," Cade said. "And you can't have any yet."

"We'll party after you get home." Herb had pulled up a chair so he could hold her hand. "Maybe not tomorrow, but soon."

"Good." Rosie glanced around the room. "We definitely need a celebration before my boys take off."

"We'll have one," Herb said. "But right now, we have a proposition for you to consider."

Lexi watched Rosie's expression as Herb described the crowdfunding idea. She seemed to be holding back any possible excitement, as if she might be afraid to hope that the ranch could be saved.

When Herb finished, she didn't say anything.

Lexi swallowed. Surely Rosie wouldn't forbid them to do this, but if she did, then they'd have to abandon the project and the ranch would be sold.

At last Rosie spoke. "Let me make sure I understand. First we have to have some worthwhile project that will get people to donate but will also produce income, like Finn's microbrewery."

Finn nodded. "Yep."

"Once we have this worthwhile project, which at this stage is a complete unknown, we then set an amount for the campaign that will pay off the loan and give us the funds to launch the project. Then we have to reach that amount by the deadline of September 1, or the whole thing falls apart and we give all the money back."

"It won't fall apart," Lexi said. "It's going to work. Chelsea was the brains behind Finn's operation, and—"

"Hey." Finn chuckled. "Not *all* the brains."

"Sorry."

"Just most of the brains," Finn said. "She knows the ins and outs of crowdfunding. If anybody can help us find the right project, she can. I should mention that there's a flexible funding option where you can keep the money if you don't meet the goal, but I know Chelsea doesn't recommend that because it looks like you don't have confidence in your project."

Rosie fell silent again, and Lexi held her breath. She glanced at Cade and he met her gaze, his expression tense.

"Well, if we don't do something," Rosie said, "we'll lose the ranch."

Herb took a shaky breath. "Yes, we will."

"I've already told myself that I can handle that, so if this doesn't pan out, we're no worse off." She gave everyone a brave smile. "So let's go for it."

Amid the cheers and the hugs that followed, Lexi kept thinking of Rosie's brave smile. What if they got her hopes up only to fail? What if the letdown affected her and she had an actual heart attack next time?

But she kept her thoughts to herself until she was driving back to the ranch with Cade in the passenger seat. Then she poured out all her misgivings about what they were attempting to do.

He listened to her without speaking. When she was finished, he sighed. "I get all that, and we're taking a risk. But we're taking a risk if we do nothing. The thought of losing the ranch literally broke her heart. What happens on the day that she has to drive away from it forever?"

"That would be awful. She's bonded to that place, I think even more than Herb is. She once told me she hoped to stay on that ranch until she turns toes up."

"Then I think that's your answer. We have to fight to keep her there. I always wondered if there would be any way I could repay Rosie and Herb for what they've done for me. This is it, Lexi. This is what I can do."

She nodded. "I know you're right, but I've never taken on such a huge responsibility before. We're meddling in their lives, trying to change the course of history."

"And what if we succeed? Wouldn't that be the greatest thing ever, to know we stepped in and found a way for Rosie to stay on the ranch until she turns toes up?"

"Yeah, it would."

Cade pulled out his phone and checked the time. "We'll have just enough time to bring the horses in and feed them before our Skype date with Chelsea."

"Right." Damon and Finn were making a beer run on the way home, so Lexi and Cade were on horse patrol. "Don't forget about Ringo."

"I won't, but let's leave him in the cabin until after the Skype call so he doesn't turn into a distraction. We'll bring him up to the house while we're having dinner."

"Damon and Finn will love that."

"Damon and Finn need to get a life."

"I know, right?" Lexi turned down the road that led to the ranch. "I understand that they both want to be financially successful, but they're sacrificing so much."

"They are, but I shouldn't make flip comments like I just did. Of course they need to get a life. We all do. In spite of what Rosie and Herb did for us, we're still damaged. The truth is, Damon and Finn don't know how to get a life. As for me, I'm…working on it."

That little speech stopped her in her tracks. She had no business comparing the guys who'd ended up at Thunder Mountain Ranch with kids who'd had moms and dads, silly arguments with siblings, bedrooms decorated with sports memorabilia and holidays with their extended family. In other words, a normal life.

She glanced at him. "For what it's worth, I think you're doing a great job."

"Thanks." He smiled and reached over to stroke her cheek. "You're right about the driving thing. I've never ridden with you, and for the first ten or fifteen minutes, it was weird as hell."

"I knew that."

"But I got used to it, and now I kinda like it. You're sexy when you drive."

"I am?"

"Absolutely. Every time you turn the wheel your breasts move ever so gently under your T-shirt. It's fun to watch."

"I'm glad that I kept you entertained."

"Oh, I was highly entertained. When your fingers curl around the gearshift, I just naturally think about how it feels when you hold on to my—"

"Don't say it." Heat sizzled in her veins. Then she groaned. "Too late. The symbolism of the gearshift is now permanently burned into my brain. Thanks a lot."

"Is that a bad thing?"

"It could be in heavy traffic!"

He laughed. "I'm not worried. You're a great driver. You won't let a little sexual imagery interfere with that. I also like to watch the way your thighs flex when you're braking or stepping on the gas."

"Stop it right now, Gallagher. You're trying to get me hot, and we have horses to round up and feed." As she parked next to the barn, she looked at the clock on the dash. "And the Skype call with Chelsea is in forty minutes."

He opened his door. "Then we'd better get moving."

Coming from anyone else, that would have been an innocent comment. But it would be hours before they were alone again, and his emotions were running hot. She suspected he had plans that didn't involve feeding horses.

When they'd dated, they'd mostly made out in his truck. But Cade's chores on the ranch usually involved working with the horses, so when she'd gone out to see him, she'd helped with that job.

That meant they'd had a few stolen moments in the barn. More than a few, come to think of it. No doubt he remembered one particularly vivid incident in the tack room when they'd been stranded in the barn during an abrupt and violent thunderstorm.

The sky was clear today, but until Damon and Finn arrived, they were completely alone on the ranch. Forty minutes. It wasn't a lot of time, but it was enough time, especially if you were Cade Gallagher.

14

CADE CONGRATULATED HIMSELF on his quick thinking in suggesting that Damon and Finn take his truck to the hospital. Riding with Lexi today had worked out to be all kinds of wonderful. For one thing, he'd tackled a prejudice he hadn't known he had and it was rapidly disappearing.

Also, the ride to the hospital and back had given him a chance to talk with Lexi. He'd stored up a powerful hunger in the past five years and whenever they were alone, he mostly thought of making love to her. But he couldn't very well do that while she was driving.

Controlling his libido long enough to have a conversation had reminded him that they used to talk all the time. It was one of the things he'd missed most. He hadn't recognized how important their discussions had been to him until he couldn't have them anymore.

But he wasn't interested in having a conversation right now. Thanks to his decision to loan out his truck, he wasn't shopping for beer. Instead he was headed into a very empty, very private barn with the sexiest woman in the world.

She walked ahead of him into the tack room and reached for a lead rope.

"Hang on a minute, sunshine." He hung his hat on a nearby saddle horn.

She turned and met his gaze. "Look, I know what you're thinking."

"Good. That saves time." He nudged the door shut with the heel of his boot and reached for her.

She stepped back. "Damon and Finn could shop really fast and get here any second."

"So what? They're not going to come looking for us, especially if the tack room door is closed." He eliminated the space between them and drew her into his arms.

"I still don't think this is a good idea."

"If you say so." He cupped her bottom and pulled her tight against his straining erection. "Your body says something different, though." He flexed his fingers in a gentle massage that always turned her on. "Your eyes say something different, too." He watched the heat build in those hazel depths. "But if you really don't want to…"

Surrender came quickly. "Oh, yeah, I want to." She pulled him down for a kiss that left no doubt that she *really* wanted to.

With encouragement like that, he instantly went to work on her jeans, but he made sure not to interrupt that red-hot kiss until he absolutely had to. Finally he had to. Hoisting her up so she was sitting sideways on the same saddle where he'd left his hat, he crouched down and yanked off her boots, her jeans and her panties. He'd love to remove her shirt and bra, but the more clothes they took off, the more they'd have to put back on. And the clock was ticking.

He lifted her back down. "Lexi, I want—"

"I want what you want."

He swallowed. Her sultry comment delivered with a knowing smile made him tremble with anticipation. She remembered. He fumbled while unzipping his fly and almost dropped the condom packet.

"Let me." She took the condom and rolled it on. "There." Turning toward the wall, she leaned over, flattened her hands against the wood and braced her legs apart. Then she peeked at him over her shoulder. "Is this what you had in mind, cowboy?"

He sucked in a breath. He'd dreamed of seeing her like this again. And here she was, her delectable little bottom thrust in the air in the most erotic invitation he'd ever known.

"Ah, Lexi." His voice was rough, his breathing rougher as he steadied her with both hands. Sliding his cock partway in, he closed his eyes and clenched his jaw against coming. The sensation was incredible, but watching it happen added another level of arousal that threatened to destroy what little control he had.

She gave a soft command. "More."

"Yeah." But he took it easy, filling her slowly, inch by inch. When he was locked in tight, he paused to catch his breath and regain at least part of his sanity. This was good. A little too good. He settled into a gentle rhythm while he fought against coming. He wanted to give her time.

Apparently she didn't need as much of that as he'd thought. Her breathless whimper was his only warning before a powerful contraction rolled over his rigid cock. With a loud groan, he abandoned himself to the demands of his body, plunging into her again and again as her orgasm brought on his.

Panting and dizzy from the impact of that orgasm, he still managed to keep them both upright as the tremors subsided.

Her laughter was shaky. "Wow."

"Yep. Wow. Think you can stand up by yourself?"

"I think I can fly."

"Me, too." He left her warmth with regret, but he took comfort in knowing they'd be back in each other's arms later tonight. If he had his way, they'd be together every night.

They'd had lots of practice making themselves presentable after a round of hot sex, so before long they were headed out to the pasture. They'd finished feeding all five horses and were walking up to the house when Damon and Finn drove in.

"We brought beer, fried chicken, coleslaw and chocolate chip cookies," Finn said as he climbed out of the truck with a bag in each hand. "How's that for awesome?"

"That's terrific. Thanks." Cade had a whole other criteria for awesome, but food would be welcome. "I didn't even think about what we'd do for dinner. Let me know what I owe you."

"Nah, we used your gas, so we're even." Damon tossed him the keys. "Thanks for the loan of the truck."

"Glad it worked out." Cade figured Damon knew the motivation behind his offer of the truck and approved of the strategy. Damon was the one who'd advised him to marry Lexi.

He would do that, too. Or at least he hoped he would. That speech of hers on the first day lingered in his mind.

It hadn't sounded like the speech of a woman who was eager for a walk down the aisle.

She might love the sex, but that didn't mean she wanted to make a lifetime commitment. Ironically, she might be thinking the same way he had been five years ago. That would be a real kick in the head if they'd mentally traded places.

"You didn't use my gas, though," Lexi said. "I want to contribute to the cost of the food and the beer."

"Sure." Damon started toward the house. "We'll do the math later. Right now we need to get on Skype. It's nearly time."

Cade pulled out his phone and discovered they had all of five minutes before they were supposed to rendezvous with Chelsea. Considering how he saw his life going, Chelsea's input was important for Rosie, the ranch and his hope that Lexi would be willing to marry him after everything settled down. He could hardly wait for this Skype thing.

At five they grouped around Herb's computer. Lexi had persuaded Finn to handle the opening comments and the introductions.

He didn't look happy about it, and he'd chosen to wear the battered old cowboy hat, but he sat in Herb's desk chair and smiled when Chelsea popped up on the screen. "Hey, Chels. We're all here."

"I see that you're there." Chelsea turned out to be a brown-eyed blonde with purple streaks in her hair and an attitude. "So what, you've gone native already?"

"It shades my eyes. There's a lot of sun in Wyoming."

"Especially indoors. I'll bet the sun's brutal in the house."

Cade glanced down to hide a smile. He didn't dare look at Lexi.

Finn ignored the dig. "Let me introduce everybody."

"And while you're at it, tell me what they do for a living." Chelsea picked up a digital tablet. "I'll make notes about that for later."

Finn went through the roster and each of them moved closer to the computer and waved at Chelsea.

When they were finished, she consulted her tablet. "I take it this is the core group."

"Yes," Finn said. "But we can recruit others, guys who were in the foster program with us."

"I hope for your sake one of them became a lawyer, because you'll need one to keep tabs on the operation. If they'll do it for free, so much the better."

Finn nodded. "There's a lawyer in Cheyenne who was here for a while. We'll get in touch with him." He seemed mesmerized by the screen. "Your hair's purple."

"Nice of you to notice." She consulted her tablet. "Major resources are—a horse trainer, a riding instructor, a renovations expert and a business owner. Oh, and you mentioned that Rosie's husband is a retired equine vet. You have a ranch in somewhat decent shape, three cabins, a washhouse behind the cabins and a barn. Does that about sum it up?"

Finn glanced around, and everyone nodded. "That's it. Oh, and Rosie's a great cook and is used to working with teenagers, but we don't want to overwork her."

Frowning, Chelsea stared at her tablet. "You need a residential program that makes use of your combined skills. Three of you know something about horses. One of you could help maintain the property, one of you can cook and understands teenagers and one of you has some experience running a successful business." Then she fell silent.

Cade heard the theme song from *Jeopardy!* in his head as they all waited for Chelsea to say something.

Finally she did. "I don't know a lot about this area, but presumably some of you do. Teenagers need help figuring out what they want to do with their lives and some of them may want to work with horses. With your personnel, you could offer a course of study that would help them decide if that's what they want."

Cade spoke up. "Is that enough of a hook? Finn got people interested in saving a building. What's our mass appeal?"

"Horses, for one. You're offering to help educate a new generation about their medical needs, their unique personalities and their use for both pleasure riding and competition."

"I can see that," Lexi said. "In the digital age, people are connecting with animals as a way to balance their lives. Horses are seen as noble animals."

Chelsea nodded. "They are. Also, parents with means would love to find out if Susie and Johnny want a career involving horses or only think they do. If you start an academy with the potential to be a prestigious training ground, then the parents will want to be in on the ground floor. That would give them bragging rights."

"I like it," Damon said. "What age are you thinking about?"

"Kids who are only a year or two away from going to college, before they have to choose a major. I'd say sixteen to eighteen."

"Both boys and girls?" Cade could see problems with a coed academy.

"I think you need to have both or risk a discrimination suit." Chelsea put down her tablet. "Hate to run out on you, but I have a date. You can email me any more questions, or we can set up another Skype time."

"We have plenty to chew on for now," Cade said. "Thanks for the session."

Everyone else added their thanks and Chelsea signed off.

"A date," Finn muttered. "I'll bet she said that to get a rise out of me. She could be going to the movies with her sister."

"Or maybe she has a date." Damon stood. "You shot her down, so she's looking elsewhere. Let's bring Ringo up here and have some dinner so we can discuss Chelsea's idea. I think it has potential."

Finn gave him a dark look. "I'll go get the cat."

Moments later, they sat around the kitchen table debating Chelsea's proposal. This time, though, Cade made sure he wasn't across from Lexi. He wanted to be within touching distance.

They'd taken some chicken off the bone and given it to Ringo in his bowl, and he was merrily chomping away. Cade doubted the cat had ever had it so good.

"I like the concept." Damon dished himself some coleslaw. "Herb has a ton of veterinary knowledge to pass on, and he loves teaching kids. Gallagher's excellent at working with horses, and—"

"Assuming he's not too distracted." Finn chuckled and picked up his beer.

"Hey." Cade skewered him with a glance. "Knock it off."

"Sorry." Finn sighed. "I'm just jealous. My love life stinks."

"It doesn't have to," Lexi said. "She still likes you."

"Chelsea? Are you kidding?"

"Nope. I watched her expression while you were talking. If you asked her out, she'd say yes."

Finn shook his head. "She's too intense. I need to focus on the business. If I could play the field like Harrison, that would be okay, but I'm not good at that."

"I could give you some pointers," Damon said. "I—"

"Thanks, but no thanks." Finn looked over at Lexi. "I'm happy for you guys, so ignore my dumb remarks. You belong together."

Lexi blushed. "Well, we, uh… We're not exactly—"

"Yeah, we do." Cade reached for her hand and squeezed it. "We always have, and I finally wised up to the fact." She didn't squeeze back, but then, she was probably busy thinking about Finn and Chelsea.

"Good," Damon said. "And this time around I'm sure you'll do the right thing. It's working out great, in fact, because we have a real ace in the hole if Lexi's teaching riding skills to these kids." He glanced at her. "Rosie says you're becoming really well-known as an instructor."

"That brings up an important point." Lexi slipped her hand from Cade's. "Are we talking about a program that would run continuously year-round? Because my clinics keep me very busy. I'm scheduled through December. You know I want to support this, but I can't teach here full-time."

"But it'd be a paying job," Damon said. "It's not like you'd be doing it for free."

"Doesn't matter," Cade said. "It'd be like us asking you to give up flipping houses and be a full-time maintenance man at the ranch."

"Good analogy." Lexi sent him a grateful smile. "I'm not saying I won't teach here at all. But I love setting my own schedule and traveling to different venues."

"And Rosie wouldn't want her to give that up." Cade felt proud of himself for adding that, especially when Lexi rewarded him with another warm glance.

"No, she wouldn't," Lexi said. "This is a promising idea, but she was very clear that none of us should sacrifice what we're doing to make it happen. If we want a full-time instructor on-site, I'll find a good one and help design the program."

Damon nodded. "Fair enough. That means three of us will be off handling our businesses and functioning as consultants mostly." He looked over at Cade. "We can't very well hatch this plan and then dump the daily routine on Rosie and Herb, so that leaves you to stay here and supervise. Are you okay with that?"

"Well, yeah, I guess so." He hadn't thought of his contribution in that way, but if it meant saving the ranch, he'd do whatever was necessary, especially since he'd stayed away so long. It was true that he had no business to run, while the rest of them did.

"That's good," Finn said, "because I think one of us needs to be on-site. We're talking about a residential program for older teens. There could be drama."

"Oh, you know there will be," Damon said. "And we can't expect Rosie and Herb to climb out of bed in the middle of the night to deal with it. They've done their share of that already."

The reality of the situation finally dawned on Cade. "Then you're saying I should live on the ranch."

Damon met his gaze. "Yes."

"Then I need a little time to think about that."

"I thought you might. But we don't have a lot of wiggle room. We have to get everything settled before Finn and I leave."

"Understood." He'd have to discuss this with Lexi later tonight when they were alone. Once he agreed to live on the ranch, he'd be locked in for the foreseeable future.

He hadn't meant to bring up the subject of marriage this soon, but it looked as if he had no choice. If Lexi accepted his proposal, he didn't relish starting married life in one of Herb and Rosie's guest rooms. A cozy cabin for newlyweds wasn't in the budget, either.

Lexi was smart. Maybe she'd have a solution. Assuming she was even remotely interested in marrying him. He wished he felt more confident about that.

15

A COUPLE OF hours later, they had a name for the project—Thunder Mountain Academy—and a tentative figure for the crowdfunding campaign, an amount that would cover the equity loan and their initial operating expenses.

Lexi found a pad of paper in a kitchen drawer and began sketching logo ideas. "Let's start with a horseshoe."

"With the open end at the top, don't forget," Finn said. "Otherwise the luck drains out."

"Spoken like a true Irishman." Damon had coaxed Ringo onto his lap, and the gray tabby purred loudly as Damon found the sweet spot behind his ears.

Lexi drew the horseshoe and arranged the initials TMA above it. "I'm no artist, but how about making the M part look like mountain peaks?"

Cade looked at her drawing. "I can see that. Good idea." He'd been fairly quiet during the discussion, as if something might be weighing on his mind.

She figured he was mulling over the prospect of living at the ranch. He'd balked a little at that idea, and she was afraid that might have something to do with her, especially considering Damon's remark about "doing the right thing" this time around.

She hoped to hell Cade wasn't going to propose. They'd been having a great time getting reacquainted, but that didn't mean she wanted to marry him.

She filled in the letters so they looked bolder. "And I know exactly who we can ask to create this logo, too. Ben Radcliffe."

"The saddle maker?" Finn looked surprised.

"Yep." Lexi glanced at the kitchen clock. "If it wasn't so late, I'd call him right now. You should see the designs he creates to embellish his saddles. He'd be perfect. We could offer to pay him, but I know he won't take it."

Damon grinned. "There's a plus. Speaking of how late it's getting, Ringo and I are about ready to call it a night."

Finn pushed back his chair. "Good idea. Do we know when Rosie's coming home tomorrow?"

Lexi tore off the sheet of paper, folded it and tucked it in her pocket. "She said if nothing unexpected happens tonight, then she can leave after her doctor shows up to release her tomorrow morning. If the doctor gets delayed, Rosie has to sit and wait, but she doesn't want us wasting gas coming to see her."

"So we'll make the place look nice for when she gets here," Cade said. "And by the way, we're not inviting a bunch of former Thunder Mountain guys to a party this week, are we? I know we talked about it, but I don't think it makes sense now."

"Nope. Not anymore." Damon scooped up the cat and stood. "But once we get our act together on Thunder

Mountain Academy, we should contact them all. They might be able to donate money or services."

A cell phone chimed with a text message. "That's mine." Finn pulled his phone from his pocket and looked at the screen. "It's Chelsea. She came up with some T-shirt slogans."

"Already?" Damon walked around behind Finn and peered over his shoulder.

"She gets excited about this stuff," Finn said.

Lexi thought Chelsea was also excited about working with Finn again, but she decided against saying anything.

Damon grinned. "These are good slogans. 'Equinimity—Definition: Good old-fashioned horse sense.' 'Raise Your EQ—Equine Quotient.' 'Never mind, it's an equine thing.' Now all we need is to get somebody to turn them into a graphic."

Lexi fished her drawing out of her pocket. "Want to text a picture of this and see what she thinks? And ask about Thunder Mountain Academy, if that name sounds good to her."

"Sure." Finn took a shot of the drawing and started typing.

"And tell her we like the slogans," Damon said. "I figured she'd be a huge asset to this campaign, but I didn't expect she'd jump right in."

"That's Chels, a bundle of energy." Finn sent off the message. "She was like that with O'Roarke's, too. Ideas flying, texting back and forth at all hours of the night." His phone chimed again. "She loves the logo concept and wants to know if we have somebody to design it."

"Tell her yes." Lexi could already picture the beautiful job Ben would do. "A talented saddle maker."

"T-shirt slogans and a logo." Cade nudged his hat back with his thumb. "It's starting to seem real."

"It is real." Lexi put her drawing back in her pocket. "We're going to make this happen."

Finn chuckled. "Chels wants to know why the hell we didn't mention the saddle maker. He should give classes."

"That's a terrific idea. Now I really wish I could call him. He's talked about wanting to pass on what he learned from his mentor, who's now retired. I love this. Chelsea's brilliant."

"I'll tell her you said so." Finn typed quickly and smiled at the response. "She wants to meet you."

"Tell her she's invited here anytime."

"Okay." Finn sent the message.

"In fact, she should come if she can get away, so she can see what she's helping promote."

"That's true." Finn looked at the screen. "She's pretty busy for the next couple of months, but she'll keep the possibility in mind. I can tell she's excited about this project."

"I'm glad," Damon said. "But I really am done for the night. See you all in the morning."

"I'll go with you. I need to charge my phone. It's almost dead." Finn stood and glanced at Cade. "You coming down to the cabin?"

"Well, I—"

"No, he's not, genius. He and Lexi have some things to discuss." Damon started out of the kitchen.

"Oh, right. I forgot. See you two in the morning, then." He followed Damon out the door.

Damon glanced over his shoulder. "I don't suppose

I could talk you into silencing your phone for the rest of the night."

"Uh, okay. I guess I could."

"Nah, don't." Damon continued on toward the front door, but his voice carried easily to the kitchen. "I hate it when you sound like that."

"Like what?"

"Like you just dropped your ice cream on the sidewalk."

"Oh, for God's sake. I don't sound like that."

They were still bickering as they went out the door.

Lexi grinned at Cade. "I'd forgotten how funny they could be."

"Yeah." He smiled briefly, but then his expression grew thoughtful again.

"Chelsea's certainly enthusiastic."

"Yep."

"I don't know if it's the project or Finn that's motivating her, but either way, Thunder Mountain Academy will benefit."

"That'll be good." He pushed back his chair and held out his hand. "Ready to take a drive, pretty lady?"

The minute she put her hand in his and let him pull her up, she felt the tension humming through him. One look into his eyes told her he had more than sex on his mind. "I should have asked you instead, since I'll be driving."

"Oh, yeah. I forgot." He gave her a sheepish grin. "Sorry. Old habits die hard."

"No worries." But that confirmed that he was distracted. They'd had a long and somewhat significant discussion about letting her drive tonight. Obviously something more important was occupying his thoughts.

She squeezed his hand and released it. "My purse is in the bedroom. I'll be right back." When she returned to the kitchen, he was standing right where she'd left him, his hands in his pockets and his head down. Yeah, he was wrestling with something, all right. His concentration was so intense he hadn't heard her come back.

"Ready?"

His head came up, and he blinked. "Yep."

They drove to their make-out spot in silence, and the longer it stretched out, the more nervous she became. Any minute she expected him to blurt out whatever was bothering him, but instead he got out the minute they stopped and came around to open her door.

"At least let me help you down."

"I'd love that." Placing both hands on his shoulders, she shivered as he gripped her around the waist with hands strong enough to support her and gentle enough to give her exquisite pleasure.

They'd perfected this routine, too. She slid down his muscular body and savored the leisurely trip. By the time her feet touched the ground, she was heated clear through by the lazy friction and the press of his hard penis against her belly.

She lifted her face for his kiss. "That was nice."

His face was in shadow and his voice was thick with emotion. "Everything with you is nice. I love you."

She hadn't expected that. She sucked in a breath.

"I love you so much, Lexi." He kissed her then, and it wasn't a hurried, eager-for-sex kiss. His mouth covered hers with care and reverence, touching down with the soft pressure of a man clearly cherishing the privilege.

She knew what to do with his lust and hunger. She could handle testosterone-fueled urges and desperate cravings. But this… She couldn't deal with this. His outpouring of love was stirring up all the girlish fantasies she'd had five years ago, and she was in real danger of letting those fantasies sweep her away. She couldn't allow that.

He raised his head a fraction. "Marry me. I was a fool to walk away five years ago. But if you can find it in your heart to forgive me, to give me another chance, then—"

"Oh, Cade."

"Then you will?" He hugged her tight. "Oh, Lexi, I promise that I'll—"

"No, I won't. Not now. Maybe not ever."

He went very still.

She ached for him, but there was no easy way to say what had to be said. "You can't come back expecting to slide right into the life we had. I don't want that life anymore."

"But you love me! I know you do!" His voice rang with anger and hurt.

"Yes, I love you. I always will. But that doesn't mean I want to become a wife to you or anyone. I used to think that love and good sex should lead to marriage."

"It should! I was an idiot not to see that before."

She reached up and cupped his face in both hands. "You're where I was five years ago. I was focused on you and our life together. But you didn't go for it, and I'm so lucky that you didn't. Your refusal forced me to take a different path, and I'm doing something I might never have attempted if you'd agreed to get married."

"What you've accomplished is terrific, and I won't get in the way of that. I swear I won't keep you from doing whatever you want."

"I wouldn't *let* you keep me from doing what I want. The very fact that you feel the need to promise not to means you still think that you have that power as a man, and especially as my husband. You'd expect me to be grateful that you didn't interfere."

He groaned. "I don't really understand what you just said."

"That's okay. But let me throw this out. You decided to move back here. Why?"

"To be with you."

"That's not enough. What do you want to do with your life, Cade? What are your goals, your dreams?"

He hesitated. "Well, I..."

She recognized that he wasn't ready to answer that question, just as she hadn't been five years ago. "It's something to think about, but there's no rush. We have plenty of time to work through all of this."

"No, we don't. You heard what Damon said. I need to live on the ranch to keep an eye on things."

"So do that. It might inspire you, lead you to some conclusions."

"But what about us? I want to be with you, make love to you and wake up next to you in the morning. Do you realize we've never done that?"

"We don't have to be married for you to sleep over." She smiled up at him. "You can do that tomorrow night if you want."

He blew out a breath. "So you love me?"

"Yes."

"And you're inviting me to spend an entire night in your apartment?"

"Yes."

"Then why the hell not marry me?"

"Take my word for it. We're not ready."

"Are you prepared to tell Damon that? Because he's determined that we're getting hitched, and the sooner the better."

"Damon? The confirmed bachelor? Where does he get off giving you advice on the subject of marriage?"

Cade shrugged. "Go figure."

"I would love to see a woman swoop in and lay him flat."

"Come to think of it, so would I. He has it coming." He was quiet for a while. "So we're not getting married."

"No."

"But I guess you still want to have sex with me."

"I do, unless you decide to get all pouty because I turned down your proposal."

"That has a certain appeal, but then I couldn't try out the bed of your truck."

"No, you couldn't. I don't have sex with pouty men."

"That settles that. I'm about to be the most cheerful lover you've ever had. I might even whistle while we're doing it."

And that was the Cade she'd fallen in love with. And being Cade, he had to carry it to extremes.

"I love these blankets," he said as he helped her spread them out. "Soft, big, colorful."

"It's dark. You can't see the color."

"I can sense color." He took off his shirt and tossed it on the tailgate.

"Oh, sure you can."

"I can." He pulled her close and reached under her shirt to unfasten the back clasp of her bra. "Your bra is white."

"All my bras are white. I don't buy colored bras."

"You did one time." He pulled her shirt over her head and threw it on top of his. "It was red." He cupped her breasts and leaned down to begin tasting.

"For prom." Her voice was a mere whisper as she closed her eyes and concentrated on the pleasure he gave her when he did this. He'd been the first boy to take off her bra, and it had been red to match her dress. Her panties had been red, too, and he'd been the first boy to slip his hand inside and fondle her, the first one to give her a climax.

After all this time, she still loved him to kiss her breasts while he eased his hand under the elastic of her panties and slid his fingers into her moist heat. He'd fumbled that first time, but he didn't fumble now. He knew exactly what she liked and how she liked it.

He used his mouth to greater advantage now, too. He'd learned to nibble and lick his way over and around, teasing her one minute and applying strong suction the next. She quivered. She moaned. And she came, faster than she used to because her body knew what to do and how to react to Cade's brand of loving.

As she trembled in his arms, he lifted her into the truck bed and pulled off the rest of her clothes. He'd become an expert at that. In moments she lay beneath him and welcomed his first powerful thrust.

With a contented sigh, he pushed a little deeper. "I love it here."

"Our make-out spot?"

"No, here, between your thighs, my belly flat against yours, my cock as far in as it will go. Here where I can feel you breathing and look into your eyes, which are this beautiful combination of brown and green."

"You can't see that, either." She wrapped him in her arms and held on. She loved it here, too.

"I can see your eyes anytime I want. I just think about you gazing up at me when we were on the dance floor at prom. No one had ever looked at me like that."

"I was wildly in love with you."

He leaned down and brushed his lips against hers. "And now?"

"Still wildly in love with you."

"You do realize you're confusing the hell out of me."

"I have faith you'll figure it out."

"I will. I have to. But in the meantime, we have this." And he began to move.

"Aren't you going to whistle?"

He started laughing, which made for an interesting sexual experience. She'd never had sex with a man who was cracking up. He'd stop pumping every so often and attempt a whistle, but then he'd laugh. Of course so would she.

Finally he paused and took a deep breath. "You have to choose which you want. I can either whistle or I can do you."

"Then do me."

"Good choice." And he proceeded to take them both on an incredible ride that ended well and noisily. Afterward he flopped to his back, gasping for air. "Told you. Screaming orgasm."

"Okay. I screamed." She struggled to breathe. "So did you."

"Nah."

"Yes." Smiling, she peered up through the pine branches where stars twinkled like Christmas lights.

After reaching for her hand, he laced his fingers

through hers. "We have to practice that whistle thing. I'll bet if I could learn to do it I'd get in the Guinness book of world records."

"Guaranteed."

He was silent for several moments. Then he squeezed her hand. "Look, I understand that you won't marry me, but if we're going to keep seeing each other, I have one condition."

"What's that?"

"I'm the only man who gets this privilege. It may be chauvinistic, but I can't deal with—"

"Done. And back at you."

He brought her fingers to his lips and kissed each one. "I'm yours, Lexi. Forever and always."

Her heart stumbled. Those were the words she'd longed to hear five years ago, the words he'd been unwilling to say. He was saying them now. Was she crazy to reject the earnest proposal he'd laid at her feet?

No. Those five years apart had taught her to be true to herself instead of reacting in a way that would please someone else. They'd allowed her to find a purpose other than marrying Cade. He needed space to discover the same thing about himself.

She'd wondered if, when the chips were down, she'd cave because she did love him so very much. Well, she hadn't caved, and she was proud of herself. She'd listened carefully to what he'd said and what he hadn't said.

He was clueless about his future except that he wanted her in it as his wife. In that regard, he viewed his role as that of a benign dictator who would generously *let* her continue to do what she wanted. She hoped he'd evolve beyond that. She would love to see him set a goal he was passionate about. But unless he could do those things, marrying him would be a huge mistake.

16

THE NEXT MORNING Cade worked alongside everyone else as they spit-shined the house. When they'd finished, they all ended up standing in the living room, as if everyone hated to sit down and dent the recently plumped and vacuumed cushions.

"So that's done," Finn said. "Now we need groceries."

"You and Damon are welcome to borrow my truck if you want to head to the store." Cade hoped they'd take the not-so-subtle hint and leave him alone with Lexi. Her rejection hurt, no matter how many times he told himself everything was okay. Making love to her was the only way he could think of to drown out the negative voices in his head.

"Whoever goes should run by Ben's shop and pick up his preliminary logo sketches." Lexi held up her phone. "He just texted me that they're done."

Damon blinked. "And you called him when?"

"About three hours ago. He's been working on them ever since."

"I have a really good feeling about this project," Finn

said. "Ben's excited, and Chelsea's on fire with ideas and—"

"Tell me about it." Damon rolled his eyes. "Did you sleep at all?"

"Some. Chels and I tossed around website concepts, and she's going to design one and see how we like it, no charge. If we agree on a logo, we should send it to her."

"She's being very generous," Lexi said, "but I think we should offer to pay her for the website design."

"She figured you'd say that, but she'll settle for food and lodging if she comes for a visit."

Lexi smiled. "I hope she does. Anyway, let's get those logo printouts before Rosie comes home. I'll bet she'd have fun helping us choose which one we want."

"I think so, too," Damon said. "Lexi, maybe you should go with Finn. You're the one who's been in contact with the guy."

"Yeah, and I'm sure Lexi won't argue about every flippin' thing on the grocery list," Finn said.

"I argued because you've gone all Pacific Rim on me! I've never once seen anyone on this ranch eat sushi. I was flabbergasted the store even carried it." Damon turned to Lexi. "Do you eat sushi?"

"Not so much."

"Cade, how about you?"

"Not my thing." He was glad to hear Lexi wasn't into it, either.

"See, Mr. Everybody Will Love Sushi?" Damon gave Finn a triumphant glance.

"Okay, okay. But you guys need to try it. I didn't think I'd like it, either, but Chels talked me into eating some and now I love it. I'll get one small tray of California rolls, and everybody can have a piece."

Damon sighed. "Fine. Go shop for sushi. Meanwhile Cade and me, we'll go muck out some stalls. It's what manly men do."

"Right." Cade had no choice but to pretend he was fine with this plan.

Lexi grabbed her purse and started for the door. "Sounds good to me. You two can get all smelly and sweaty while Finn and I roam the grocery store's air-conditioned aisles."

After they left, Cade walked with Damon to the barn. "Was that on purpose or did it just work out that I lost my bid to have some time with Lexi?"

"A little of both. I did want to ask you something when she wasn't around. Did you talk to her about the idea of you living at the ranch?"

A sharp pain lodged in the vicinity of his heart. "Sort of. Turned out to be a nonissue."

"How come? I thought that was why you hesitated about making a commitment, so you could discuss it with her first."

"It was. I asked her to marry me, and she said no."

"No?" Damon stopped walking and turned to stare at him. "That woman's crazy about you! Why would she turn you down?"

Cade shrugged. "I don't really get it, either." But he needed to get past the sick feeling in his gut. After all, she'd said she loved him. And she still wanted to have sex.

"Well, color me shocked." Damon blew out a breath. "Wait a minute. You said she might make you suffer as payback for when you walked away from her. Maybe that's what this is all about. Revenge."

"I wish I could believe that, but I can't. It was the

nicest rejection a guy could have. She still wants to hang out with me. She invited me to spend the night at her apartment."

"With her in it?"

"Of course with her in it, doofus. What else?"

"I dunno. Maybe she's asking you to housesit when she goes out of town. Water her plants. Feed her fish."

"No."

"Well, if I were you I'd clarify that. You don't want her thinking you're some pathetic errand boy." Damon peered at him. "And wipe that whipped-puppy expression off your face ASAP. I swear you and Finn are perfect examples of why I'll never fall in love if I can possibly avoid it."

Cade smiled. "Good luck with that."

"I've dodged the bullet so far. Or the arrow or whatever the delivery system is these days."

"It feels like you've been struck by lightning."

"Oh, that's appealing, getting fried with a gazillion watts of power. Sign me up." Damon shook his head. "Come on, Romeo. Let's shovel some shit."

It was the perfect activity for Cade's present frame of mind. Filling a wheelbarrow with manure and rolling it out to the pasture was a repetitive yet satisfying task. Sweating and using his muscles felt good.

Not as good as making love to Lexi, but when he was doing that, he wasn't thinking at all. Mucking out stalls allowed him to think. Much as he longed to turn off his brain, that wouldn't help him figure out how to handle this situation.

No matter which way he looked at his relationship with Lexi, he kept coming to the same conclusion. He needed to back off. Sure, he wanted to spend the night at her apartment. They'd never made love in a bed, and he'd give up almost anything to do that. Anything but his self-respect.

Damon had made a good point about not looking or acting like a whipped puppy. Or a lovesick one, either. He'd been concerned about Rosie when he'd first arrived, but once that crisis had begun to resolve, he'd focused almost entirely on getting Lexi back.

Well, he had her back, in a sense. But this time he was the needy one, not her. He didn't like facing that truth, but there it was in all its embarrassing glory.

Her words kept running through his head. *You're where I was five years ago.* But that couldn't be right. He'd grown and matured, which was why he was ready for marriage. The idea of settling down with Lexi didn't scare him anymore. He was eager to be a good husband and, if they had kids, a good father.

Maybe he hadn't been able to pop out an answer to her question about goals and dreams, but he had them. They'd begun forming when he'd set eyes on her after all this time. He wanted to build a life with her in this place where they'd met and fallen in love.

That's not enough. Maybe not to her, but for him it was huge. He'd been drifting, marking time. He hadn't admitted it to himself then, but he realized it now. Seeing Lexi again had inspired him with a new vision of how things could be.

It would have been so simple if she'd said yes to his proposal. Together they'd figure out where to live so that he could keep track of everything at Thunder Mountain Academy. Maybe Damon would build them a little house that wouldn't cost a whole lot.

But she'd said they weren't ready for marriage. He

couldn't imagine being more ready. He wanted her with him, end of story. They got along, and the sex was amazing. How much more did anyone need to be happy, for God's sake?

On his last trip to the pasture with the wheelbarrow, Hematite wandered over to say hello. Cade was touched by that and wished he had a carrot in his pocket. But he had nothing, so he began humming "Red River Valley" to see what would happen.

Hematite came closer and stretched his neck to sniff the front of Cade's shirt.

Cade used the tune of "Red River Valley" but substituted his own words. "Come and stand by my side if you love me. Do not hasten to leave me alone. Just remember the cowboy who saved you, and the haven you now call your home." He smiled. Not bad for composing on the fly.

He sang the verse again, and Hematite bumped his chest. When he stroked the horse's neck, the gelding stayed put, as if enjoying the caress. Still singing, Cade walked around so he could lean against Hematite's rib cage. The horse didn't seem to mind. His ears flicked back to indicate he was listening to the song, though, so Cade kept crooning away.

Meanwhile he draped himself all over that animal, putting pressure on various parts of the gelding's body. Hematite remained where he was as if this was normal behavior for both of them. It almost seemed as if the horse had *missed* him.

Maybe he had. At the Circle T, Cade had been a constant presence in Hematite's daily routine. It hadn't been like that recently, though. He'd been too involved with Lexi.

Giving in to an impulse, he gradually maneuvered the horse over to the fence. He propped one foot on the lowest rail and eased his other leg over the gelding's back. Other than a ripple of his glossy coat, Hematite didn't react.

Cade moved slowly, inching his way astride as he continued to sing his bastardized verse of "Red River Valley." Hematite had never had a rider on his back, at least not for long. Cade had accustomed him to the saddle, but Thornwood might have ruined all that work.

And yet…Hematite didn't flinch as Cade slowly settled his weight on the gelding's back. He was on, still singing, his thighs loosely gripping, his hand wrapped in a section of the horse's dark mane. He tightened his thigh muscles, and Hematite moved away from the fence.

Cade didn't give a rip where the horse went as long as he didn't start bucking. He didn't. Instead he made a circuit of the pasture as if on parade.

Continuing the song became tough because he wanted to laugh. This goofy horse had never been ridden. Yet to look at him sedately cruising the perimeter with Cade on his back, anyone would think he'd been carrying people around all his adult life.

A flash of color at the gate alerted Cade to the fact that Lexi stood there in her turquoise T-shirt and jeans. She gave him a thumbs-up, and he returned it. Then he figured he'd pushed his luck about as far as it would go and quietly slid to the ground.

Hematite stopped and turned his head to look at Cade as if asking what else this strange human had in mind.

"Nothing more today," Cade said. "But thanks for the ride, and I'm sorry I've been neglectful." A wisp of an idea drifted through his mind, but with Lexi standing over there waiting, he was too distracted to concentrate on it.

Yet he vaguely realized that the idea was connected to Hematite in some way, and if he came back out here on a regular basis, he might find some answers. He stroked the horse's silky neck. "We'll do this again tomorrow." Then he went to fetch his empty wheelbarrow and push it over to the gate.

Lexi opened it and smiled at him. "Red-letter day, huh?"

"Yeah. It was the weirdest thing. I almost felt like he'd missed me." He rolled the wheelbarrow through the gate.

"I'll bet he did. I'm sure he knows you're the one who took him away from the bad place." She fastened the latch, and they started toward the barn. "Rosie called. They're on their way."

"That's terrific. I'm sure both of them can't wait to sleep in their own bed again." Not surprising he'd think of that. Beds were on his mind today.

"She mentioned that very thing. They've had it with hospitals, although she praised the staff to the skies. But she's ready to come home."

Cade walked a little faster. "I just might have time to shower and change before they get here."

"Rosie wouldn't care. She's used to smelly cowboys."

"Hey! Be nice."

"I am being nice. I'm used to them, too."

He responded to that soft comment with a surge of warmth. Only minutes into their conversation and he wanted her. He flashed back to the morning he'd come into the cabin after his shower to find her tucked into his bunk without a stitch on. No wonder he'd neglected his horse after that.

While he thought about sex and how it tended to make him stupid, she continued to talk. He finally started paying attention when she asked him a question.

"Do you think we should wait on the logos?"

"Until when?"

"Until she seems rested enough to talk about it. She and Herb want to know what we've been up to, but she sounded a little tired on the phone. Going through the discharge process might have worn her out. We don't want to push it her first day back."

"God, no. Whatever happened to her, we don't want a repeat, and too much excitement could send her right back."

"That's what Finn and Damon said, too."

He glanced over at her as they reached the barn. She was so beautiful it made his throat hurt. Sunlight frosted her curls and brought out the rich shades of brown, rust and copper. Her cheeks were tinged with pink. He hoped that came from being close to him, horsey smells and all.

Her breathing seemed unsteady, too. "Of course I'll stay as long as everyone needs me to."

How about forever? He didn't say it.

"But I'm guessing Rosie should take a nap at some point. I'll probably head on home then. I need to get back to some of my clients who've texted or emailed." She took a slip of paper out of her jeans pocket and handed it to him. "Here's my address. You're welcome to come over tonight if you want."

Oh, he wanted to. He wanted the pleasure she offered so much that it was like ambrosia on his tongue. He had to force the next sentence out. "Thanks, but I'm going to hang around here."

She looked startled. "Is that because I—"

"It's because of everything—being with the Brotherhood, keeping Herb and Rosie company, talking about the future of the ranch. But mostly it's because I need to think, and when I'm with you, my brain checks out."

She exhaled slowly. "I'll miss having you there, but… you're probably doing the right thing. I'll save the wine and candles for next time."

"You planned a celebration?" To hell with thinking things through. "Then I'll—"

"No." She stepped closer and reached up to brush a bit of debris from his cheek. "Follow your instincts. I'm in this for the long haul. One night doesn't matter."

"Easy for you to say." His gaze lingered on her mouth.

"Not easy. But I admire your decision to stay here tonight. And your ability to gentle an undisciplined horse." Her eyes sparkled with mischief. "And your talent for whistling."

"No fair. Now you're playing dirty."

Instantly she looked contrite. "I am and I'm so sorry!"

"Don't be. I love it when you tease me. I love that you planned a private party for us. I love *you*."

She swallowed. "I love you, too. I'm glad I got back in time to watch you riding Hematite. You looked… happy."

"You bet I was happy. He trusted me enough to let me up on his back. That's a great feeling, when you earn the trust of an animal that's been abused."

"I'm sure it is." She held his gaze. "You might want

to consider—" But instead of finishing the sentence, she looked away and muttered something under her breath that sounded like, "Shut up, idiot."

"What? What might I want to consider?"

"Nothing. Ignore me. You'd better go take your shower." Rising on tiptoe, she gave him a quick kiss before heading to the house.

He stared after her in confusion. She'd been about to give him her opinion, something she'd never been shy about doing. They'd been discussing Hematite, so the comment she'd stifled must have had something to do with the horse. Why censor it?

Maybe she'd decided that she didn't know enough about training horses to offer an opinion. No, that didn't fit. She would have just said that. Instead she hadn't wanted him to know what she was thinking.

He knew better than to pester her about it. If she hadn't told him now, she wasn't going to. But trying to figure it out on his own would drive him crazy.

17

AN HOUR LATER, Lexi sat in the ranch's cozy living room sipping a beer and watching Herb's and Rosie's joyous expressions. At last they had what they'd longed for—their three favorite boys back home at one time. Everyone else had a beer except Rosie, who preferred Baileys and had decided to give herself a few more days before indulging in anything alcoholic.

She reposed like a queen in the room's most comfortable easy chair beside the hearth, her feet propped on an ottoman to show off her bright red toenails. Early this morning a manicurist and a hair stylist from her favorite salon had shown up at the hospital to give her, as Rosie phrased it, a tune-up.

Consequently her hair was styled and her nails polished. The minute she'd come home she'd changed into a lightweight lounge outfit in a warm blue that matched her eyes. She'd insisted on hearing every detail concerning Thunder Mountain Academy and had one of her boys in mind to handle the legal angle.

She'd been eager to discuss the logo, and they'd eliminated all but two of the designs. Rosie held them up.

"Which one, then? The brown horseshoe with the green letters or the black horseshoe with deep blue letters? Other than the colors, they're pretty much the same. The green *M* might look a little more mountainish, but the blue is good, too."

"I like the brown and green," Cade said from his perch on the arm of the couch. "I've always liked that combination." He smiled at Lexi, who sat at the opposite end of the couch.

She returned his smile. He'd been the first guy to fall in love with the color of her eyes. Come to think of it, he'd been the first guy to fall in love with her, period, not counting Jason Phelps in sixth grade.

Cade was the first guy she'd fallen for, too, not counting Jason Phelps, who'd thrown her over for Emmy Leech in seventh grade. Not long after Jason's defection, Rosie had brought Cade home to Thunder Mountain Ranch, and life hadn't been the same since.

Lexi couldn't imagine loving anyone the way she loved Cade. But oh, how she wished she'd kept her mouth shut earlier, down by the barn. At least she'd caught herself before finishing her thought.

Passing out unwanted advice was a bad habit. And in this case, she could have potentially interfered with a process that was Cade's alone. Just because she saw an obvious path for him didn't mean she should blurt it out, or that he should take it. He had to work this out for himself.

Finn sprawled on the couch's center cushion, his booted feet propped on the coffee table. Its surface was marred with the imprint of many boot heels. "I think the black with the blue is more of an attention-getter and it'll show up the best on a T-shirt."

"I'll go with Finn on this one." Damon had brought a kitchen chair into the room and straddled it while he sipped on his beer. "It's bold. I like bold."

"I like the brown and green." Herb occupied the other easy chair on the far side of the hearth. "It's softer, but it seems more academic." He glanced at Lexi and Rosie. "Ladies?"

"I like the brown and green," Lexi said. "It makes me think of growth, and that's what we want to achieve for the kids who come here."

Rosie turned both logos around and gazed at them. "And I like the black and deep blue, because it makes me think of thunder and rain, which seems a heck of a lot more dynamic than seeds sprouting."

"Wouldn't you know?" Herb glanced around in obvious amusement. "We're split down the middle. Anybody want to change his or her vote?"

"We should ask Chelsea," Lexi said.

"I'm on it." Finn left the couch with surprising speed. In minutes he'd photographed both logos and texted them to Chelsea. "I predict she'll vote for the black and deep blue."

"Good call," Damon said. "Any woman with purple streaks in her hair will want the bold statement."

Rosie laughed. "Finn, are you involved with a woman who has purple hair?"

"We've worked together, but we're not *involved*."

Damon cleared his throat. "Couldn't prove it by me. When it walks like a duck and quacks like a duck, usually it's a—"

"Stuff it, Harrison." Finn concentrated on the image captured on his phone. "You know what? We could add a lightning bolt to the black and deep blue, but it wouldn't look right with brown and green. Another reason to go with the black and deep blue."

"A lightning bolt." Damon's gaze settled on Cade. "Sure you don't want to change your vote, Gallagher?"

"Nope." He drained his bottle. "I don't see this academy as a lightning-bolt situation." He got up and offered to fetch more beers.

Lexi watched him walk into the kitchen, his lean-hipped stride taunting her with possibilities she wouldn't be enjoying tonight. He was gorgeous. Any woman would be lucky to—

"Lexi?"

Rosie's voice broke into her X-rated thoughts. "What?"

"I'm not sure what your plans are, but you're welcome to stay over tonight."

"Thank you, but I really need to get home." She wondered if Rosie had caught her staring longingly at Cade. Probably. Rosie didn't miss much.

"Okay. I just… Well, you've been a big help and you just seem…to belong here."

Yep, Rosie was still matchmaking. "That's a lovely thing to say. I—"

"Chels likes them both!"

Grateful for the interruption, Lexi glanced at Finn. "Equally? But we need to pick one, so what now?"

"I guess we have a little time. She wants to test them on some marketing people she knows and see which gets the best response." He looked up from the screen. "You all okay with that?"

"Sure," Rosie said. "I don't care if she's dyed her hair every color of the rainbow. The woman obviously knows something about promotion."

"She definitely does." Finn's proud smile revealed a lot, probably way more than he intended.

Damon, of course, had to point it out. "I give you exhibit A." He gestured toward Finn. "The boy is besotted."

"Am not."

"Are so."

"I love it." Rosie gazed at them fondly. "It's like old times listening to you two bicker. But much as I'd love to stay here all afternoon and be part of every deep discussion, it's time for me to retire to the bedroom and take a nap. I need my beauty sleep."

Her announcement created a flurry of activity. Amid hugs and well wishes, Rosie disappeared into her bedroom. That was Lexi's cue to leave, too. Her overnight bag was already in her truck. The adventure, at least the part where Rosie had scared them all to death, was over.

Cade offered to walk her out, and she accepted. She couldn't shake the idea that after today, everything would change. She might have fantasized that Cade would spend his days here and his nights at her apartment, but after his decision not to come over tonight, she wasn't counting on that.

When they reached her truck, she turned to face him with a sense of inevitability. This felt like a much bigger goodbye than it logically should be. He'd be here, and she planned to visit often.

He braced a hand against her door and shoved back the brim of his hat. "I desperately want to share your bed tonight."

She gulped. "I know."

He traced a finger along her cheek, down the curve

of her throat and into the vee of her shirt. "I think you want me there, too."

"Yep."

His gaze searched hers. "When I came back, I couldn't think of anything but making love to you."

She couldn't help smiling. "I was pretty focused on that myself."

"I'm glad you were. I'm glad we had the chance to find out the chemistry's still there. I guess it always will be. I'm counting on it, in fact."

Her breath caught. "Why?"

"Because I've made a decision, and it feels right to me. I won't make love to you again until I figure out what I'm supposed to do with my life. You were right about the dreams and goals. But when you're in my arms, you become my dream and my goal. I can't think beyond that."

"I get it." Was she disappointed? Oh, yeah. But she knew exactly what he was talking about.

"Then there's this business with my new relatives. I don't have a handle on that, either. I've promised to go over to the Last Chance Ranch with you next month, and I dread it."

"I know you do."

He sighed. "Bottom line, I need time alone to think things through."

"That's perfectly understandable."

His green eyes were filled with regret. "It could take a while."

"I hope it doesn't take five years." She'd meant it as a joke, but he looked horrified.

"Dear God, no! But I don't... I can't say exactly how long..."

"I know." Her heart ached for him, for them. "But when you do figure it out…"

"You'll be the first one I tell." He leaned in. His kiss was filled with love and anguish.

As she clung to him, she memorized the velvet touch of his mouth and the passionate thrust of his tongue. She didn't know how soon she'd be back in his arms, but the wait was guaranteed to be tough. And much too long.

As the days went by, Lexi saw Cade whenever she went out to the ranch, but he made sure they were never alone. She sat through a farewell dinner for Finn and Damon without exchanging a single private word with Cade. She had a feeling he'd told everyone about his decision because no one asked questions.

While she didn't want to imagine what that discussion had been like, she was grateful that their relationship hadn't been a dinner topic that night. Talk about Thunder Mountain Academy had dominated the conversation instead. The brown-and-green logo had tested best, even with the addition of a lightning bolt to the black and deep blue. Chelsea was almost finished with the website.

Once she'd completed it, they'd pick a date to launch the project on the Kickstarter platform. Damon had taken inventory of the renovations necessary and had decided they needed to build a fourth cabin so they'd have a greater number of beds to offer. He'd blocked out two weeks in July to come back and tackle the work.

Cade's cousin Molly had been recruited to set up a curriculum. Lexi would oversee the riding lessons built into it, although she wouldn't be the on-site teacher.

She'd made a list of candidates she'd approach in the next few weeks.

The dinner had ended, and she'd hugged both Finn and Damon, who were flying out the next day. She hadn't hugged Cade, and he hadn't offered to walk her to her truck. The distance between them was tough to deal with, but she hadn't expected a quick resolution. He had a lot to work through.

She forced herself not to count the days since she'd last touched him, held him close and made love to him. But she knew they were mounting up. Her clinics absorbed her attention whenever she conducted them, but in her free time, she searched for excuses to go out to the ranch. She told herself she went to see Rosie and check on progress with the academy.

Good thing, because if she'd driven out there to see Cade, she would have been disappointed. He was always busy with the horses. Rosie and Herb didn't discuss Cade with her anymore, and that felt strange, too. She felt excluded from some grand plan, but she knew he had to accomplish this without her.

Finally, *finally*, she received a text from Cade.

Can you meet me at the corral tomorrow at ten?

Her adrenaline level spiked and she texted back one word—Yes. His timing was good. Her next clinic was two days away, but she'd secretly hoped he'd show up at her door for the big reveal. She'd imagined a passionate celebration in her apartment.

Yet did it matter in the long run how or where he unveiled his new program? If he'd discovered something significant about what he wanted from life, then any time was a good time to hear about it. He'd chosen the corral for their meeting. That likely meant his plan involved horses, which was promising.

She didn't sleep much that night and she was ready to leave her apartment way too early. After cleaning out her email inbox she played computer games until the clock on the screen told her she could leave. *Thank God.*

Once on the road, she had to control the urge to speed. If she got picked up, she'd be late, and if she didn't, she'd be early. But driving at the speed limit was agony.

When she pulled up beside the barn, Rosie and Herb were both leaning against the railing of the corral. She expected a more private moment, but this was Cade's show, and if he wanted them there, he should have them there.

They both turned and came over to embrace Lexi.

"He's so excited," Rosie said. "I'm glad you were available."

"Me, too."

"If you hadn't been, he was going to reschedule," Herb said. "He mentioned that he didn't want you dropping everything to accommodate him."

"Oh." She put a hand to her chest, which felt tight with emotion. He'd listened. He'd really listened. "That's...very sweet."

Rosie put her hand on Lexi's arm. "He loves you."

She swallowed. "I love him, too."

"Then you'll both be fine." Rosie squeezed her arm. "Here he comes."

She turned, and Cade walked out of the barn leading a fully saddled Hematite. His smile dazzled her as much as it had years ago when they'd been teenagers.

"Hey, Lexi."

"Hey, Cade."

"Can somebody please open the gate?"

Herb responded, moving quickly to open it. Lexi was too transfixed by the sight of Cade leading his glossy black horse to do anything but stare. She knew what he intended to do, and he was her hero.

Once he'd led Hematite into the corral, he spoke quietly to the horse. No singing this time. Obviously they were past that. Then he put his foot in the stirrup and swung easily into the saddle.

Hematite stood like a carved statue. Then Cade nudged him into a walk. That forward motion was interrupted when he asked Hematite to back up. The horse responded without question.

With a full heart, Lexi watched Cade take Hematite through a trot and a mellow canter. The horse easily changed leads and stopped on a dime. The gelding that had never been ridden until a few weeks ago now responded to Cade's every request.

But Cade wasn't finished. He dismounted. "Lexi, want to try him?"

"Yes, please." She stepped through the gate and walked over to Hematite. First she stroked the horse so he'd become used to her scent and her voice. She glanced at Cade. "Has anyone else ridden him besides you?"

"No, but he'll be fine. I wouldn't let you get up on him otherwise." He held her gaze. "Lexi, this is what I'm supposed to do."

"Train horses?"

"Not just that. Rehabilitate the ones who've been abused. Who better than me? I get them."

She sucked in a breath. "That's perfect."

"And it's the funniest thing, but now that I know that about myself, the Chance family isn't so scary anymore."

"Makes sense to me. You've found your life's work. That has to be empowering."

He smiled. "Apparently it is. So climb aboard. Test him out."

Mounting the black horse, she felt the power radiating through him. As she took the reins and started around the corral, he was the perfect gentleman.

"You're a sweetie," she murmured, and the horse's ears swiveled back to catch the sound of her voice. "And the guy who trained you is also a sweetie. You're lucky to have found each other."

Hematite snorted as if acknowledging that.

"Now let's see what you can do." She urged him to a trot and then to a canter. Whirling around the ring on Cade's trusty steed, she rejoiced in his triumph. He hadn't wanted to train a horse that only he could ride. Hematite had to be safe for the person he loved most. For her.

At last she eased the horse back to a trot and a walk. Then she stopped in front of her audience of three. "Anybody else? He's a great horse."

Rosie laughed. "Thanks, but Herb promised to help me make potato salad for lunch. You're both invited, so come on up when you're ready." She hugged Cade. "Fabulous job."

Herb hugged him, too, and then he slung an arm around Rosie's shoulders as they returned to the house.

Dismounting, Lexi waited until Cade opened the

gate. Then she led Hematite through. "Back to the barn?"

"That works." He fell into step beside her. "Before I get carried away, and I'm liable to, I have something to say."

Her heart beat faster. "Cade, this is a wonderful breakthrough, but I hope you're not thinking that it means—"

"That you'll accept my proposal? Nope. That's what I wanted to talk about. I won't propose again."

She gave him a startled glance. "You won't?"

"No. Don't get me wrong. I still want to marry you, but I'm leaving it up to you. When you think we're ready, pop the question."

"Well, that's…unexpected."

"Any problem with it?"

"No! I'm pretty sure I'll love the idea. I just have to adjust my thinking."

He laughed. "If you need any help with that, I've become an expert."

"No doubt." They'd reached the hitching post outside the barn, and she paused. "Mind if I park this horse here for a second?"

"Okay, but I thought you'd want to head right into the barn so we could unsaddle him. Rosie and Herb will have lunch ready any minute."

"So no fun and games in the tack room?" She hadn't thought so but wanted to make sure.

"Nah, we've outgrown that. I think we're ready for a real bed."

She looped the reins loosely around the hitching post and turned to him. "Tonight? My place?"

"I was hoping you'd ask."

She launched herself into his arms. "Hoping I'd ask? I've been going crazy!"

"That makes two of us." He gathered her close. "Thanks for waiting for me."

"I would have waited even longer."

He smiled down at her. "Well, you didn't have to. And by my calculations, that leaves us all kinds of time to love each other."

She nestled against him. "I like the sound of that."

"Me, too." His mouth sought hers.

As she reveled in the secure warmth of his arms and the familiar heat of his kiss, she sensed a subtle difference, a solid confidence that had been missing before. After a lot of hard work on his part, Cade Gallagher finally knew who he was.

Epilogue

Sitting around a campfire waiting for the steaks to be done felt like old times to Rosie, except for the fact that she'd been told to leave all the work to Lexi and Cade. They'd come up with the idea of grilling over the fire pit down by the cabins, but they'd insisted that Herb and Rosie allow themselves to be waited on. Herb seemed fine with it, but Rosie preferred being useful.

"Mom?" Cade called over to her. "You still like your steak medium rare?"

"Yes! Good memory!"

He flipped the steaks with a long-handled fork. "Then yours will be ready pretty quick."

Rosie got up from the bench she'd been sharing with Herb. "I'll get my plate."

"I'll get it," Lexi put down the tongs she was using to toss the salad. "You relax."

"Lexi, sweetheart, I've relaxed enough to last me the rest of my life." She was halfway over to the bench where they'd stacked the plates and utensils when her cell phone belted out the dwarves' working song from *Snow White*.

Cade laughed. "Who did you assign that ringtone to?"

"Damon." Rosie smiled as she pulled her phone from her pocket and put him on speakerphone. "Hi there! You should be here. We're cooking steaks over the fire pit."

"Wish I was! Who's there?"

"Just me, Herb, Lexi and Cade. What's up?"

"Well, the two weeks I'd planned to be there just got shortened. I have a buyer for this house and should've had it almost finished by now, but the tile company shipped the wrong color. I can get the right stuff, but not until after the Fourth, which screws up the schedule."

Rosie frowned. "Don't stretch yourself too thin trying to make it up here."

"I won't. I just can't be there as long, but I'll be there."

Lexi stopped messing with the salad and came over to listen, hands in her pockets. She looked worried.

Rosie gave her a smile of reassurance. "Any time you can spare would be great. Don't stress over it."

"I'll try not to. I can squeeze in six or seven days around the Fourth, because I can't do anything here without the tile, anyway. But after that I have to come back and finish up. The buyer's desperate to move in."

"Are six or seven days enough time to build the cabin?"

"Maybe, but I might need some help."

Muttering something under her breath, Lexi pulled her phone out of her pocket. Then she tapped the screen and held it toward Rosie with a mischievous smile.

Rosie could barely keep from laughing. That would be some matchup—Philomena Turner, sole proprietor of Phil's Home Repair, and Damon Harrison, house-flipper extraordinaire.

"Tell him I can help." Cade wandered over, fork in hand. "But he knows it's not my strong suit."

Still thinking about Phil as a possibility, Rosie nodded. "Cade can—"

"I heard," Damon said. "That's great, and I'll take it, but I was wondering if you know somebody with good construction skills who'd work cheap."

Lexi jiggled the phone in front of Rosie. She'd typed a quick message: in exchange for riding lessons.

Leaning down, Cade peered at the screen. "So who's—"

Lexi pressed a finger to his mouth and shook her head.

"Actually," Rosie said, "I do know someone, a good carpenter and a trained electrician who'd probably work in exchange for riding lessons."

Lexi nodded enthusiastically.

"Is he competent?"

Lexi rolled her eyes, and Rosie almost lost it. This was going to be fun.

"Damon," Cade said. "Phil is—"

"Extremely competent." Lexi glared at him and made a slicing motion across her throat.

Cade's eyebrows lifted.

"Great," Damon said. "Give me his email address, so we can talk about what needs to be done. We can plan out our schedule before I even get there. That will save time."

"I'll do that." Rosie was trying so hard not to giggle, and she didn't dare glance at Lexi. "Gotta run. My steak's ready."

"Enjoy. Love you."

"Love you, too." She disconnected the call.

Lexi grinned and shook her head. "Classic."

"I know!" Laughing, Rosie tucked her phone in her

pocket and headed for the stack of speckled blue tin plates that were a ranch tradition for cookouts. "This is going to be hysterical. But I'd better get my steak before it's burned to a crisp."

"It won't be." Cade walked over to the fire and speared her steak. "I moved it away from the heat when Damon called." He placed it on the plate she held out and then added a foil-wrapped potato. "So you're not planning to tell him Phil's a woman?"

"We're not," Lexi said. "And don't you, either."

"Why?"

"I've got this one." Herb had been quiet through the entire exchange, but now he rose from his bench and walked over to the fire. "They're not telling him because he leaped to the conclusion that his helper would be a guy."

"Yeah, I know he did, but with a name like Phil—"

"I didn't tell him her name," Rosie said. "You did. I just said I knew a person who was a good carpenter and electrician. He made the chauvinistic assumption all by himself. Springing Philomena on him should make him rethink his prejudices."

Cade's eyes widened. "You're setting a trap?"

"Out of love, sweetie." Rosie patted his cheek. "Only out of love."

* * * * *

*Nautical archaeologist Avery Walsh knows former
navy SEAL Knox McLemore will hate her when he learns
the truth. But she can't resist the heat between them!*

Read on for a sneak preview of
IN TOO DEEP,
a **SEALS OF FORTUNE** novel by *Kira Sinclair*.

"Keep looking at me that way and we're going to do
something we'll both regret."

Avery jerked her gaze from Knox's bare chest to his
eyes. "How am I looking at you?"

"Like you want to run that gorgeous mouth all over me."

"Hmm…maybe I do." She could hear her own words,
a little slow, a little slurred.

"You're drunk, Doc."

Flopping back onto the sand, Avery propped her head
against Knox's thigh.

She stared up at him, his head haloed by the black sky
and twinkling stars. They both seemed so far away—
Knox and the heavens.

"I've never gotten drunk and made bad decisions
before," she said. "Was hoping we could make one together."

He made a sound, a cross between a laugh, a wheeze
and a groan. "What kind of bad decision did you have in
mind?"

"Oh, you know, giving in to the sexual tension that's
been clawing at us since the day we met. But I guess
you're not drunk enough yet to want me."

"Trust me when I say I don't have to be drunk to want you, Avery."

She made a scoffing sound. "You don't even like me."

Slowly, Knox smoothed his hand across her face, fingers gliding from cheekbone to forehead to chin.

"I like you just fine, Doc," he whispered, his voice gruff and smoky. The words spilled across her skin like warm honey.

He growled low in his throat. His palm landed on her belly, spreading wide and applying the slightest pressure. "I'm fighting to do the right thing."

"What if I don't want you to do the right thing?"

She felt the tremor in his hand, the commanding force weighing her down. If he stopped touching her she might float off into the night and never find her way back.

"I don't take advantage of women who are inebriated." His words were harsh, but his eyes glowed as they stared down at her. Devoured her.

Never in her life had she felt so…desired. And she wanted that. Wanted him.

"Please."

Avery was certain that in the morning she'd hate herself for that single word and how close she sounded to begging. But right now, she didn't care.

"Please," she whispered again, just to make sure he knew she meant it.

Don't miss
IN TOO DEEP by Kira Sinclair,
available July 2015 wherever
Harlequin® Blaze® books and ebooks are sold.

www.Harlequin.com

HBEXP0615